"I'm going to have you...sooner or later," Chase murmured.

With a grin he tugged Jamie's lower lip between his front teeth. A second later he stole her breath with a kiss, his tongue teasing her mouth open. With gentle pressure he rubbed his chest against hers, drawing her nipples into hard peaks. She shifted, a soft gasp letting Chase know she'd felt his erection straining for release. *Soon, very soon...*

Jamie whimpered as heat pooled in her lower body. He did something terribly wicked with his tongue then, thrusting inside her, then pulling back as if showing her exactly what he wanted to do to her. Goose bumps covered her flesh as vivid pictures came to mind. Chase naked—oh, lordy—thrusting into her over and over, making her scream.

His lips moved to her ear. "I'm going to taste every inch of you," he warned, his hot breath making her shiver. "And I'm going to give you pleasure you've never even dreamed of."

Sooner, Jamie thought, *please make it sooner...*

Blaze™

Dear Reader,

This month marks the launch of a supersexy new series—Harlequin Blaze. If you like love stories with a strong sexual edge, then this is the line for you! The books are fun and flirtatious, the heroes are hot and outrageous. Blaze is a series for the woman who wants *more* in her reading pleasure....

Leading off the launch is bestselling author Vicki Lewis Thompson, who brings us a heroine to remember in the aptly titled #1 *Notorious*. Then popular Jo Leigh delivers a blazing story in #2 *Going for It,* about a sex therapist who ought to take her own advice. One of today's hottest writers, Stephanie Bond, spins a humorous tale of sexual adventure in #3 *Two Sexy!* Rounding out the month is talented Julie Elizabeth Leto with the romp #4 *Exposed,* which exposes the sexy side of San Francisco and is the first of the SEXY CITY NIGHTS miniseries.

Look for four Blaze books every month at your favorite bookstore. And check us out online at eHarlequin.com and tryblaze.com.

Enjoy!

Birgit Davis-Todd
Senior Editor & Editorial Coordinator
Harlequin Blaze

GOING FOR IT

Jo Leigh

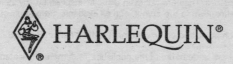

TORONTO • NEW YORK • LONDON
AMSTERDAM • PARIS • SYDNEY • HAMBURG
STOCKHOLM • ATHENS • TOKYO • MILAN • MADRID
PRAGUE • WARSAW • BUDAPEST • AUCKLAND

To Birgit Davis-Todd for her faith, insight and friendship.
This is just so cool.

ISBN 0-373-79006-6

GOING FOR IT

Copyright © 2001 by Jolie Kramer.

This edition published by arrangement with Harlequin Books S.A.

® and TM are trademarks of the publisher. Trademarks indicated with
® are registered in the United States Patent and Trademark Office, the
Canadian Trade Marks Office and in other countries.

Visit us at www.eHarlequin.com

Printed in U.S.A.

A NOTE FROM THE AUTHOR...

Everyone says you shouldn't do it. The sane thing would be to drop it. Why risk it? Why take a chance you might get creamed?

Oh, what the hell...GO FOR IT.

Sound familiar? I hope so. I don't know about you, but most of the truly remarkable moments in my life have started out with that nervous tickle deep inside, with the challenge to step out of my comfort zone.

I had an incredible time writing my first Blaze novel. Creating two characters like Jamie and Chase was a definite challenge. They're both gutsy, strong, successful... and completely confused about love.

But, and here's the important part, they both threw caution to the wind. They went for it. They took the biggest, scariest risk of all—they dared to love.

My wish for you is that you, too, GO FOR IT. Take that risk. Put your heart on the line. *You'll never know unless you try.*

Jo Leigh

1

DR. JAMIE Talks Sex...and Manhattan Listens!

Darlene Whittaker took a deep drag of her cigarette outside the offices of WXNT Talk Radio and stared at the face on the billboard across the way. Dr. Jamie Hampton was the newest "It" girl in Manhattan, the topic of conversations from the Bowery to the Bronx. Beautiful, brilliant, radical Dr. Jamie.

Darlene hated the no-smoking laws in New York that had forced her outside and cursed the mayor and all the voters at least once a day. She missed her local bar, where she used to drink tequila shooters with beer chasers and go through about a half a pack a night. Damn, those were good times.

She was here on a hunch. The article had been her idea. It was also her idea to interview Dr. Jamie on the air. The good doctor hadn't wanted to, but her station manager Fred Holt had insisted. Holt was many things, but stupid wasn't one of them. The national exposure Dr. Jamie would get with the article was going to help get her syndicated, and that's where the big bucks were. Dr. Laura, Howard Stern, Delilah—they all made a fortune for four hours on the air, five days a week. Nice work if you could get it.

Unless, of course, Darlene's hunch was right, in which case the ensuing scandal would get Dr. Jamie a one-way ticket to obscurity, and Darlene about ten grand more per article.

She just wished she could be sure.

She focused on the billboard again. Even fifty feet wide Jamie still looked tiny. Didn't the woman know the waif look was dead? With that short dark hair and those huge dark eyes, she came across as Little Miss Innocent—which was the hook. Just like the sign said, she talked sex and Manhattan listened. Straight answers, no euphemisms, no giggling. She told women they could have sex like men, and the women were eating it up. She had the number-one show in her market, and she was the number-one topic around watercoolers and in lunchrooms.

Darlene snorted. She'd seen 'em come and go, and Dr. Jamie wasn't going to be around very long. She was like a pet rock or a lava lamp. A sparkler on the Fourth of July. The trick for Darlene was to catch the light while it flared and turn the sparkler into a Roman candle. Darlene would be the one to light the match, and Jamie would burn.

Jamie's eyes, almond shaped, deep brown, with what had to be fake lashes, stared down from the billboard with all the innocence of a lamb before the slaughter. When Darlene was through with her, Jamie would be knocked off that perch of hers and she'd have to face life among the great unwashed. Hell, Darlene was doing her a favor. Toughening her up for real life. Especially life in New York City.

God bless research. If Darlene hadn't found Jamie's old roommate in college, if she hadn't gone all the way to Buffalo to do the interview in person, if Dianna Poplar hadn't dropped just enough hints about the sex doctor…this article would have been about as interesting as a night at the Laundromat. But a scandal—that changed everything. That sold magazines. And that meant the kind of money Darlene deserved. The kind that would get her out of her hideous apartment and into something decent.

That she was able to dethrone the current queen of New York was an extra bonus. The cherry on top. Jamie was so much like all the girls Darlene had gone to college with—beautiful, bright, successful without any effort. What had Jamie done, really, to deserve this job? Gotten her degree? Big deal. Darlene had a degree, and she wasn't about to go on the radio and say she was an expert on sex.

Jamie was a fraud. And Darlene was going to prove it.

The roar of a beefed-up motorcycle caught her attention, and she watched a guy on a Harley glide into a brilliantly lit parking space next to the Dumpster. She couldn't see much of him—just his leather jacket, the worn jeans, the boots and the black helmet. But as she stared, he got off the bike, took off his helmet and shook his hair free. It was longish, below his collar. Then, as if he sensed her watching him, he looked over. She was too far away to see the details of his face, but she knew who he was.

Chase Newman. The race-car driver. Another one of the beautiful people who showed up at all the right parties and were paraded on the pages of magazines like *Vanity Fair* with other gorgeous rich people. She happened to know that *People* had tried to dub him Sexiest Man Alive, and he'd told the magazine to go to hell. She had to give him credit.

He turned to lock up his bike, and the short hairs on the back of her neck rose. It was her own personal radar system. There was a story here. What, she didn't know yet. But the short hairs were never wrong.

She narrowed her gaze as she studied him. The way he moved, the way he stood, shouted confidence, sensuality, raw male energy. The kind of charisma that beguiled the most jaded hearts. Even she hadn't been immune. She'd met him at a fund-raiser—some kid thing, or maybe pets. She'd wanted to do an article on him then, but she couldn't find a hook. If she could figure out a way to combine the Dr. Jamie story with a guy...especially a guy like Newman.

She'd seen it before, although not terribly often. Mostly there were wannabes, men who swaggered and flexed and flashed their money around for all to see. But when the real thing came along, everyone knew it. There were some men who commanded attention. Respect. Who made a person want to breathe the same air, or at the very least stand in their shadow. Who owned the room, and all the women in it. The ladies fell in love with a man like that after even the briefest exposure—like it was some kind of virus. She'd seen it a thousand times. Women falling all over themselves to be near a man with that kind of charisma. Believing some of it would rub off on them.

Oh, yeah. Chase Newman would be perfect to put into this piece, if only she could find a way. Something about Chase and this station niggled at the edge of her consciousness. What was it? As she reached for another cigarette, she glanced at her watch and swore. She'd better get inside. Dr. Jamie was waiting. She hurried inside to the smoke-free air of the most popular talk-show radio station in the five boroughs, New Jersey and parts of Connecticut, Massachusetts and Vermont.

"Okay, boys and girls," Dr. Jamie Hampton said into the mike. Her favorite mug was filled with green tea, and her notes were stacked neatly in front of her. "With me now is Darlene Whittaker, from *Vanity Fair* magazine. She's going to interview me right here, right now, up close and personal. And a little later, you'll get your chance to ask me some questions, too." She turned to her guest, outfitted with fresh coffee and her own set of headphones. "So, Darlene. What can I tell you?"

"You're a lot younger than I thought you'd be."

God, she was tired of that comment. "Twenty-seven on my next birthday."

"Is the title real? Or does your first name happen to be 'Doctor'?"

Jamie laughed, already hating the woman. It wasn't Whittaker's looks. She'd dressed in Manhattan gothic, with horn-rimmed glasses, a head of curly, unkempt black hair, a black tunic over black jeans, and red lipstick so bright she probably stopped traffic. The look was too passé, but that wasn't it. The way Whittaker looked at her was another story. Something wicked was brewing inside the reporter. Something devious. "The title is real. I got my PhD in human sexuality at NYU."

"When?"

"Two years ago."

"At twenty-four?"

"Yep. I started college at sixteen, got my master's degree at twenty-one."

"Wow. That's some accomplishment. So, it was while you were a doctoral candidate that you started the radio show on campus?"

"Right. *The Sex Hour.* We broadcast from the campus radio station, and the show got pretty popular."

"Isn't it true that the reason you were so popular is that you're a female version of Howard Stern? Outrageous just for the sake of shocking your audience?"

"Well, I suppose that could be true if one considers the truth shocking."

"The truth?"

"I talk about sex. With all the weirdness that implies. Kinky sex, normal sex—whatever that is—solo sex, monogamous sex, safe sex. Sex on the beach, and in the kitchen."

"And the Woman's League of Decency has tried to shut you down because all you do is promote sex to teenagers."

"I wouldn't know about the Women's League of whatever, but I do know our demographics. Most of our listeners are in their twenties and thirties."

"The attempt to get you off the air has been in all the papers for the past six months. Don't you read the *Times?*"

"I skip over the boring articles."

Whittaker gave her a sarcastic smile. Damn Fred for making her do this. Sure, she wanted to be syndicated, but the show should speak for itself.

"When was the last time you talked about chastity?"

"Two days ago. I encouraged a caller to keep her knees together unless she was walking. Does that count?"

"But then tonight you taught a woman how to masturbate!"

"Someone had to."

"What are all the religious leaders going to say?"

"Thank you?" Jamie looked through the five-inch plate-glass window in front of the room, and met the gaze of her producer, Marcy Davis. Marcy's left brow arched as she fought a smile. Then Cujo, whose real name was Walter Weinstein, gave her the signal to go to commercial. "We've got Darlene Whittaker here from *Vanity Fair,* doing a live interview. This is Dr. Jamie, and we'll be right back."

She turned to her guest as she took off her headphones. "Having fun?"

Whittaker extracted her headphones from the forest of black hair. "Do I have time to go to the john?"

"Sure do. We've got a whole five minutes of commercials."

Whittaker crossed the room and struggled with the heavy soundproof door. Once she was out, Marcy walked in.

"So far, so good."

After checking to make sure no microphones were live, Jamie turned to her producer. Marcy was the best, and Jamie thanked the radio gods every day that Marcy had been the one to bring her over to WXNT. At forty-two, she bitched about being the old lady of the station, which was technically true, but no one cared except Marcy.

"You know," Marcy said, "I really like her sense of color. She's a summer, don't you think?"

Jamie put her finger to her lips. "She could be right outside the door."

"So what?" Marcy fell into the guest's chair. "This was a stupid idea."

"You won't get an argument from me."

"You're doing great. But I don't like that it's live. It's not fair."

"Since when did fair enter the picture? Either she'll

write the truth or not. In the grand scheme of things, it doesn't really matter, does it?''

Marcy shook her head. "Of course it matters. This is radio, sweetie—where numbers rule the day and the only thing you can count on is change. You need this article to be good, or at least provocative. A good scandal wouldn't hurt at all.''

"Oh man, you're serious, aren't you.''

Marcy nodded, but something in the other room had captured her attention. Jamie knew what it was as soon as she glanced over. Ted Kagan, the DJ who came on after Jamie, was talking to Cujo. Ted was a sweetheart, and it didn't hurt that he was also deliciously gorgeous. Marcy hadn't ever said anything, but Jamie knew beyond a shadow of a doubt that her producer had the hots for him. And Jamie also knew that Marcy wouldn't do anything about it because Ted was thirty. As if that mattered. Love was love and, unless one of the participants was under eighteen, age didn't mean squat.

"Marcy?"

She didn't respond. Not for a few seconds at least. Then she turned to look at Jamie. "What?"

"He's a doll, isn't he?"

Marcy's cheeks got pink. "Who?"

"Okay. Have it your way. But you do realize I'm an expert on relationships."

Marcy stood up. "Right. And let's see...your last relationship was when, exactly?"

"A person doesn't have to die to be a pathologist."

"Nice analogy, except that it has nothing to do with the subject at hand. I've known you over a year, missy, and I haven't seen you go on a date even once.''

"I've been busy.''

"Busy, my *ass*. You're a workaholic, and you know it."

Jamie relaxed. She could live with that diagnosis. "I know. And I'm trying to ease up. It's difficult."

"That's another load of garbage. Have you made any plans for your vacation?"

She shook her head.

"Well, if you don't, I will. I'm thinking Tahiti."

Jamie glanced at her panel. She donned her headphones and pressed her on-air button. "Welcome back to WXNT. I'm Dr. Jamie, and I'm being interviewed by Darlene Whittaker of *Vanity Fair* magazine. But first, are you tired of waking up with a sore back?"

Marcy sighed as she pulled open the booth door. It seemed to get heavier every day. Just as she got it open wide enough to walk through, Whittaker turned the hall corner and rushed past her without so much as a thanks. Rude, rude, rude. But then, so many people were these days.

She glanced in the production booth. Ted was still there. God, he was so yummy. Tall, slender, blond—he had the words "golden boy" written all over him. He was also one of the nicest men she'd ever met, and if she didn't stop dreaming about him, she'd have to shoot herself.

It didn't help that his divorce had come through two months ago, and that he was actually starting to show some interest in dating. She'd never survive watching him parade sweet young things through the office.

She really should ask him out. Just take the bull by the horns. Put it all out on the table. Jamie was always talking about how women let fear stop them from having fun. That they should have the same opportunities as men when it came to recreational sex. And that there was no point in beating around the bush. If she wanted to hop in the sack with Ted, she should simply walk up to him and ask. Go for it, as Jamie was so fond of saying.

Oh, please. She could barely look at the man without blushing like a twelve-year-old.

She sighed as she headed toward the production booth door. The phones would start lighting up any second, and she wanted to get a real good mix on the line.

Ted was looking at a newspaper when she walked in, and he didn't even glance at her as she took her seat by the phone. The computer to her right was her link to Jamie. Once she got a caller, she'd type the name, age, location, and the gist of what he or she wanted to say. Most nights, the phones never stopped. Tonight was no exception, which was good. She needed to be too busy to think. She slid on her cordless phone receiver and pressed line one.

DARLENE KNEW she was losing ground. Dr. Jamie was a lot more poised than she should have been, especially at her age. Twenty-six, and already the top-rated DJ in New York. Shit. At twenty-six, Darlene had been in college, an English major with no boyfriends, no girl-friends, and an eating disorder.

Of course, Jamie was prettier in person than in her publicity photos. Pouty lips, perky tits and, come on, couldn't she at least have one pimple to even the score? No. Pimples were for women like Darlene. In the article, she'd probably describe Jamie's skin as alabaster. Flawless. The *bitch*.

"If you don't mind, Darlene, I'm going to take a call."

Darlene nodded, wishing she'd had a chance to smoke during that last commercial.

"This is Lorraine from Queens." Jamie hit a button, and Darlene could hear a little static on the headphones.

"Dr. Jamie?"

"That's me. Do you have a question?"

"Yeah, well. Yeah."

"Go on. I don't bite."

"The other night, you were talking to Kelly from Pt. Washington about how she got seduced by this guy—"

"She *let* herself be seduced."

"Yeah, well, that's the part I wanted to talk about."

"The idea that no woman can be seduced unless she wants to be?"

"Yeah."

"Okay."

"I don't know. I mean, there's this guy at work. Steve. He is so gorgeous, and he's funny and sexy. You know what I'm talking about. He's one of those men who can have any woman he wants."

"No man can have any woman he wants."

"But, like, I've got a boyfriend, and I don't mean to say I did anything with Steve, but I sure thought about it. I don't like to admit it, but if he'd asked, I'd have said yes."

"Why? What is it about Steve that makes him so irresistible?"

"I don't know. He's really good-looking."

"So you'd have sex with all really good-looking men if they asked you?"

Lorraine laughed. "No."

"Then it must be something else."

"Okay. The way he looks at a person. It's like, uh, I don't know. It's like he sees right inside me."

"Great. He knows how to focus. Have you slept with every man who focused solely on you?"

"No. But that's mostly 'cause no one ever has. Not like Steve."

"I admit, being paid attention to is flattering, but it's no reason to drop your drawers. What else?"

"I don't know. I swear. It's just a combination of things, I guess. The way he walks and smiles. When he comes into my office, I can hardly breathe. It's like he's magic or something."

"He's not magic. He's just self-assured. He knows he can make women swoon, so he does."

"I'll say."

"Here's the thing, Lorraine. If you wanted to sleep with him, far be it from me to tell you what to do. Go for it. If you don't want to sleep with him, don't. But don't lie to yourself and say you were *seduced*. There's no such thing. Seduction is an excuse for behavior you know is inappropriate."

"It's a pretty damn good excuse."

Now it was Jamie who laughed. "Just be strong. Know you have a right to choose. Tell the truth to yourself and you'll be fine."

"So, you've never been seduced?"

"Nope. I haven't. Not even once."

Darlene got a little shiver, and said, "You don't think chemicals have anything to do with it? Pheromones? That a woman can get swept away?"

"No. Absolutely not. I do think there can be a chemical connection between people, and that attraction exists and can be very strong. But the idea that a woman is helpless to fall into a man's arms is ludicrous. Relationships, even brief ones, should be about making choices, and about honesty.''

''And you don't think falling in love could just happen.''

''No, I don't. I think that's one of the biggest myths in our culture. Lust can happen in an instant, although it doesn't have to be acted upon. Love only comes with time and work. It's a woman's choice whether she wants to have sex or not, whether she's married or not. It's your body. Respect it. Take care of it. Give it a treat now and again. And if you don't have anyone to help you, do it yourself, with or without help from toys. I'll bet there are a lot of married women out there right now who wish they'd listened. Who waited to see if the man who seduced them was actually a man they wanted to live with forever. Given the dismal marriage statistics, I'm willing to wager that for at least fifty percent of the women, they didn't look before they leaped.''

Darlene felt those hairs stand on the back of her neck again. She had it. The perfect article. The perfect hook. ''Let me get this straight. You're saying that no man, no matter who he is, can seduce a woman?''

''That's right. Not if a woman is honest.''

''No amount of charm, charisma, sex appeal could have any effect?''

''Not if a woman doesn't want to be seduced. Have you ever looked up the word? I have. According to the dictionary, *seduce* means 'to induce to have sexual intercourse.' What I'm suggesting is the idea that no one can be induced. If it's forced, then it's rape. If it's consensual, it's not seduction. It's an excuse, nothing more. No woman can be seduced without her permission. Period.''

Darlene closed her eyes for a second, just to calm herself. "How would you like to put your money where your mouth is?"

Jamie's brows came down. "What do you mean?"

"Exactly that. You say no woman can be seduced without her permission. I say fine. Prove it."

Jamie laughed a little. "There's no way to do that. Every woman has to come to that decision for herself."

"But there is a way to prove it." Darlene's heart hammered in her chest. This was so great. "Here's what I want to do. I'm going to set you up with a man who's seduced his fair share of women. More than his share. You two are going to spend time together. He's going to lay on the charm. And then we'll see what happens."

"I'll tell you exactly what will happen. Nothing."

"I don't think so."

"It's ridiculous. There's no way I can be seduced."

"You're on. I think you don't know what you're talking about. And we're going to see who's right."

"Hey, yeah, Dr. Jamie," Lorraine said, reminding Darlene that she was still on the line. "That would be so cool."

"What would be cool?"

"Well, like, for you to show us. To prove it."

Darlene held back her whoop of joy. This was even better than she could have hoped for. "Right. Walk the walk instead of just talking the talk."

"Hold on." Jamie looked at her with utter exasperation. Darlene didn't give an inch. Jamie turned back to the mike. "Lorraine, I wish you luck with your guy, and thanks for calling." She punched line two. "This is Dr. Jamie. Did you have a question?"

"Yeah," a deep baritone voice said. "I think you

should do it. And I volunteer to be the guy. I could seduce you, baby. And it wouldn't take no two weeks.''

Darlene leaned back. This was great. Just great. The article would write itself.

Jamie shook her head in disbelief as she pressed the next button. ''How about line three. Pam from Chelsea?''

''Come on, Dr. Jamie. You could report every night. You know, give us an update. A blow-by-blow. Tell us what it's like out there in the real world. We could all learn something. You're always telling us to go for it. Now it's your turn.''

''Thanks for sharing.'' She punched the next button so hard it almost broke. ''Debbi from Yonkers. Do you have something else you'd like to talk about?''

''Uh, well, yeah.''

Jamie's shoulders relaxed. ''Great.''

''I think, you know, that you shouldn't be the one to give the nightly reports. The guy should. Or you should do it together.''

Jamie's head fell into her hands. But then she sat up again. ''This is Dr. Jamie, and we're talking about sex. We'll be back after these commercials.'' Then she threw her headphones on the desk.

Dr. Jamie wasn't on such solid footing now. Darlene leaned back as she took off her own headphones. Her gaze went to the production booth and Marcy Davis. The woman wasn't looking so smug, either. The two of them were Barbie dolls, and Darlene wanted to make them squirm. Marcy turned to look at the door as a man walked into the other booth. Perfect. It was Chase Newman, the inspiration for this adventure.

He spoke to the board operator for a moment, then

he turned so she could see his face. Good God, he was stunning. Fabulous jaw, dark brows over smoky, intense eyes. Just the right amount of five-o'-clock shadow. Now, *he* was an expert on sex. There was no question the man was a maestro in the bedroom. Those lips alone could send any woman over the edge.

She was a freakin' genius. This was *perfect*. Dr. Jamie didn't stand a chance. And wouldn't it be fun when all of New York watched her fall on her perky little ass. He just had to be willing to play along. Darlene would make sure he was willing.

JAMIE TRIED to smile at Whittaker, but she couldn't. She wanted the reporter gone, the interview finished, her show over, and this nonsense dismissed. Where was Marcy? She should be riding to the rescue, dammit.

Whittaker did her a favor and left the room. At least Jamie could be grateful for that. But where was Marcy? Jamie's program was going up in smoke, and Marcy had decided to take a brief vacation. Jamie was going to have to kill her. In the meantime, though, she'd better get ready to sway this conversation another way. This was her show, dammit, not Darlene's.

Damn! Cujo's signal to her was desperate. She had no idea how long she'd been stewing. "Welcome back. This is Dr. Jamie Hampton, and we're here with Darlene Whittaker from *Vanity Fair*. Let's talk about *your* lives. Is there a question about your body you've always wanted to ask? How about sex? Come on, guys. Masturbation. Cross-dressing. G-spots. Don't be embarrassed."

All the lines were blinking, but according to Jamie's computer, Gabby Fisher was on line one. God bless her little neurotic heart. Gabby was a regular, and she wasn't shy about taking air time. She'd fill up a good ten minutes. Just as Jamie was about to press the button, Whittaker struggled through the door and hurried to her seat.

Jamie shoved the button down, terrified by the gleam in Whittaker's eyes. "Gabby, hi."

"Hi, Dr. Jamie."

"What can I do for you tonight?"

"I think it would be great to have you show us, you know, how to be strong with a man."

Jamie cursed silently. This wasn't going to go away. "You already know how to be strong. You don't need me to show you."

"I might know how," Gabby said, her voice dejected, "but it never works out that way. I guess I'm just not like you."

"You can be whatever you want to be, Gabby. You just need to shift your beliefs about yourself. A stunt like this isn't going to show you anything."

Whittaker moved her chair closer to the desk. "Are you afraid, Dr. Jamie?"

"No, not at all. But my expertise is in helping others. This isn't about me."

"But don't you think it should be?"

"What, so all surgeons should remove their own gallbladders, just for the experience?"

Gabby laughed.

Whittaker didn't. "I think you're hiding behind that title, Jamie. I think you don't want to put your money where your mouth is."

"You're right. In this instance, I don't."

Whittaker's gaze shifted to the window, then back again. "It would make a hell of an interesting experiment. I know your listeners would learn a lot. Show them firsthand what happens when a man is out for seduction. See what happens. Instead of talking about the experiment, go into the lab.''

Jamie forced herself to keep calm—to not reach over and strangle the reporter. ''I just don't believe this is the kind of thing one can demonstrate. It's not like baking a cake.''

Whittaker smiled at her, then turned to the mike. ''Well, audience, are we going to let her off the hook? I'll tell you something. My magazine wants this information. All the women in New York want this information. This could be the most important radio program ever. Or, Dr. Jamie, were you just blowing so much smoke?''

''I don't blow smoke. Ever.''

''Then, that leaves only one option.''

Damn her to hell and back. Marcy was going to pay for this. And so was Fred Holt.

Jamie leaned in to her mike. ''I'll tell you all about options…right after these commercials.''

She saw Cujo jump at the unexpected change in the schedule. But he was on top of things, and a second later Big Al's Furniture Mart announced a super, super, super sale.

She made sure her mute button was on, then turned to Whittaker. ''What the hell are you doing?''

The reporter smiled so smugly that it was an invitation for a whack. ''My job. Just like you're doing your job.''

''You know this isn't the kind of thing one can demonstrate. You're talking about a publicity stunt.''

''Not necessarily. It could be very educational. If any of it's true. Is it?''

"Yes, it is. But I don't intend to be anyone's guinea pig."

Whittaker shook her head. "Want to bet? If you don't do it, I'm going to smear you and your radio show into the dirt. I know that Independence Broadcasting is looking at buying your show for national syndication. And I know that one way or another, they're going to be influenced by this piece I'm writing. So the choice is yours. Play ball, or find yourself a new job."

"Why are you doing this?"

Whittaker smiled. "Because I can."

Jamie caught Cujo's hand signal out of the corner of her eye. She turned back to the mike, fuming. She wouldn't be blackmailed. Not by this witch. Marcy would tell Whittaker what she could do with her stupid idea. But right now, Jamie had to keep control of her broadcast. "Welcome back."

The production booth door opened. Fred Holt and Marcy walked in. Marcy looked panicked. Fred turned to face Jamie, his jaw set and his gaze filled with dollar signs. It didn't take a rocket scientist to get the gist. Fred wanted this to happen. He wanted his station to be number one and stay number one, and as far as he was concerned, Jamie was his ticket. But surely even Fred Holt could see this was a stupid prank. He wouldn't be manipulated by this crazy woman, would he?

Cujo flapped his arms at her, then pointed at the phone lines.

Dammit! "Gabby, you still there?"

"Yes, I'm still here. And I'm really glad you're going to do this, uh, thing. But maybe you could explain what it is you're going to do."

Whittaker leaned forward. "Here's what she's going to do. She's going to go out on a date. On a whole bunch of dates. Just like she was you or me. Only, she's gonna show us how it's supposed to be done. How a woman can't be seduced."

"Wait a minute. This has been fun, but come on. I don't even have a boyfriend right now so—"

Whittaker leaned into the mike. "That's not a problem."

Jamie's stomach turned. "What does that mean?"

"You'll see."

"Tell you what. Write whatever you want to in your magazine. I'm not playing."

"And disappoint all your loyal fans?"

"My fans are smart enough to realize that there is no such thing as seduction, so I've already won."

Darlene turned smugly toward the production booth. "Oh, really?"

Jamie didn't want to look, but she had to. Oh man. It was worse than she'd thought. Fred Holt had moved to the window. His face was very, very pink. His gaze nearly singed her eyebrows. This was no joke. Behind him, Marcy threw her hands into the air. So much for her help.

Jamie looked at the door. She could get up and walk out. That's all. Just walk out. But that would mean giving up her show. She loved her show. Her show was her whole life. The only thing she'd ever done for herself, by herself. And who was she kidding? She wanted syndication every bit as badly as Fred did. A national show would be the kind of achievement no one could deny—the money, the prestige, and proof she'd made the right life choice by turning her back on her parents' medical practice.

Jamie turned to the Wicked Witch of the West Side. "All right. I'll do it. But I'll pick the guy."

"Sorry. No can do. I pick the guy. You don't want to be accused of fraud, do you?"

"Whoa. No. No way. I'm not—"

Whittaker stood up and went to the door. This time, she opened it as if it weighed ounces instead of pounds. A man stood on the other side. He walked into the booth, which immediately shrank to half its size. Jamie swallowed, trying to figure out where all the air had gone.

He stepped into the light and everything stopped, including her heart. He was quite simply the most gorgeous guy she'd ever laid eyes on. He was sex on legs, the devil in blue jeans, trouble with a capital *T*. He was all that and a shot of Tabasco.

"Jamie Hampton," Whittaker said, leading him to the mike. "This is Chase Newman. The man who can't seduce you."

"Holy f—"

Cujo lunged for the button and, for the first time in a year-and-a-half, there was a full twelve seconds when the five boroughs, New Jersey and parts of Connecticut, Massachusetts and Vermont heard nothing but dead air.

2

CHASE FOUGHT A SMILE. He was actually enjoying Jamie's reaction, the way her big brown eyes widened, the pink flush on her cheeks, how she nervously licked her lush upper lip. He'd seen her before when he'd come to the station, but they'd never spoken. In fact, she'd been frightened of him, moving to the far side of the hallway when he'd passed, sneaking looks at him, blushing, like now. The last time, about six months ago, he'd almost asked her why, but she'd ducked into the ladies' room.

He liked her show, even though her message was a bunch of garbage. It was a smart move on Fred's part to have hired her. The station hadn't had a major ratings winner in a long time. Not that he cared. This wasn't his thing anymore. His father had owned the station, and Chase had inherited it after the old man died. But he wasn't a part of it now. The only reason he came here was because they gave him a small office where he collected his business mail, and let him use Fred's secretary for some clerical work now and then. Not having a permanent residence, it was convenient.

He saw Cujo signal that the commercials were about to end. Jamie didn't look ready. Damn, she was a pretty thing. Innocent. At least she looked innocent, which all of New York knew wasn't true. But she sure seemed flustered as hell. She was known for her no-nonsense approach to matters of the body, for her unflinching answers to the most kinky questions. No one would mistake her for a silly female. Yet right now, she looked like a twelve-year-old with her underpants showing.

Darlene grabbed hold of him and pulled him toward one of the guest chairs. "Chase, why don't you sit down." The booth had been recarpeted since the last time he'd been in it. That had been years ago. Now, it seemed smaller, but like every other booth he'd seen— the thick carpet to mask sound, an oversize desk for the DJ and several mikes for group discussions. The console was computerized, a far cry from the equipment in place when his father had first started the station.

Darlene sat in the chair next to him. She gave him a set of headphones and found one for herself. Jamie just kept staring at him, and he wondered how long it would be before she blinked.

His attention went back to the other side of the glass where Cujo was waving wildly, trying to get Jamie's attention. Dead air was trouble. Chase decided to give her a break. He pressed the button to turn the guest mikes live.

Darlene caught on. "This is Darlene Whittaker from *Vanity Fair*. In case you've just tuned in, I'm interviewing Dr. Jamie for a feature article..."

Chase tuned her out as she explained the situation to the audience. He probably should have listened, given his role, but he was preoccupied. Jamie hadn't spoken yet. She'd run a hand through her short hair, making it a little messier than she'd probably intended, but he wasn't complaining. He liked seeing a preview of what she'd look like in his bed, hair tousled, cheeks flushed, trying to catch her breath.

There were two things that mattered to Chase. Racing and women. Not necessarily in that order. The pursuit of his two hobbies took equal amounts of time and energy. They were very similar, in fact. Both cars and women needed careful attention to make them purr. Truth be known, cars were the easier of the two. They never got emotionally involved.

"Chase, why don't you tell the listeners something about yourself."

He nodded, not taking his eyes off Jamie. "I drive cars. Sometimes, I live in New York."

"Yes, well, uh, you drive race cars, isn't that right? And didn't you win at Le Mans last year?"

"Yeah."

"And weren't you also dating Charlize Theron at that time?"

"Yeah."

"What happened?"

"She wanted a relationship."

"And what about you?"

"I was good in bed."

Darlene laughed, and Jamie's blush deepened.

He leaned over and took Jamie's right hand. It was fisted, and she tried to pull it away, but he didn't let her. "Jamie," he whispered, "what are you afraid of?"

She jerked her hand away, and in that act of defiance she seemed to gather her wits about her. She cleared her throat, moved her chair forward, adjusted her headphones. "Tell me, Mr. Newman. You seem to be a busy man with a full life. Why on earth would you want to do this?"

Good. She was back to her feisty self. "I don't have any plans for the next couple of weeks."

"You don't have any plans," she repeated. "Did you hear what Ms. Whittaker said? If we go through with this nonsense, we'll have to see each other every day. You'll have to come in to the studio and give progress reports." She shook her head. "You don't think this is completely nuts?"

"It's weird as hell, but I'm game," he said.

"There has to be more of a reason than your lack of a busy schedule."

"Why?"

"Because this is... It's absurd!"

"Is it?" Darlene asked. "Is it absurd when you tell Noelle from Brooklyn that she's not really in love with her boyfriend? Is it absurd when you teach Cindy from Queens that she's weak and spineless because she couldn't say no?"

"I never said she was spineless. Besides, that's different."

"Why? Because it's not *your* life on the line? Because *your* heart isn't at risk?"

Jamie turned her gaze to Darlene, and Chase was surprised the writer's hair didn't catch fire. This was not a mutual admiration society. These women were out for blood.

Maybe he'd been too hasty. What sounded like a laugh a few minutes ago was becoming complicated. He didn't do complicated. On the other hand, Jamie had that luscious mouth.

Darlene touched his shoulder. "Chase, have you ever seduced a woman?"

"Yep."

"How many?"

"All of them."

Darlene grinned. "So you think you can seduce Dr. Jamie?"

"Yep."

Jamie's eyes looked like they were ready to pop. "Are you serious? Every woman just falls into bed at the crook of your finger? Obviously that statement is a gross exaggeration."

"No, it's not."

"What, you're so fabulous, no woman can resist you?"

"No woman I'm paying attention to. I don't know all that much about the world, and I am, after all, only a guy who drives cars, but I do know what women want, and how to give it to them."

"Oh, please. That's the most arrogant crock of—"

"How long do you think it'll take Jamie to succumb?" Darlene asked, barely masking Jamie's curse.

He chuckled. "I don't know. It depends on how willing she is to play her part honestly."

"Explain that, please."

He turned from Darlene to Jamie. "She needs to walk into this with no prejudice. It has to be real—as if I asked her out and she said yes of her own free will."

"Jamie, how do you feel about that?"

"I think this joke has gone far enough." She lifted her cup with shaky fingers, then put it down again without taking a sip. "Why don't we hear from some listeners. Mr. Newman, thanks for being such a good sport, but you can go now."

"Not on your life," Darlene said, her tone as sharp as a knife blade. "There are only two ways this is going to end. Either you're going to come in here in two weeks, in front of Chase and all your listeners, and tell us you stayed strong, that he didn't seduce you, or you're going to admit you're a fraud.''

"Ms. Whittaker, I invited you here as a courtesy. I agreed to be interviewed. I didn't sign up to be made a laughing stock.''

"Oh, I'm not laughing. I'm dead-on serious. Because, Dr. Jamie, I don't believe you've ever been with a man like Chase. I don't think you've been with a real man. Because if you had, you would know that sometimes the mind takes a back seat to the body. You're just like the rest of us poor slobs, babe, and you know it. You're playing with your listeners' hearts, and their lives.''

"I take what I say seriously. I've got a PhD in human sexuality. I've dedicated my life to this work.''

"But you don't even date! You can't tell us you understand what we go through if you're safe inside your radio station. It's time to put up or shut up, Dr. Jamie.''

Chase watched Jamie look through the window as she abruptly gave the station identification, not even trying to respond to Darlene's diatribe. Fred Holt stood with his nose practically pressed against the glass. He didn't look happy. The woman—what was her name?—the producer, was freaking out. She was yanking on Fred's coat sleeve. Chase's old buddy Cujo was grinning like the cat that ate the canary. Chase knew why, of course. Ratings. This little experiment would be a ratings monster. The Arbitrons would go through the roof.

He hadn't been involved with radio since he was a teenager, despite his father's wishes—but he knew the game. He knew what it took to be successful. His father had never understood that he found it all boring. He would never be at the mercy of numbers. Chase needed physical challenges. Excitement. The unexpected.

He turned to the lovely doctor. She still looked flushed, but the pink in her cheeks was fueled by anger now. She was trapped, and she didn't like it. It would be a challenge to get through her defenses—to weaken her resolve. Of course, he could do it. There was no doubt. Not because he was Don Juan, but because women wanted to be seduced.

He understood the game, and he was an excellent player—probably because he knew he had nothing to lose. It was never going to develop into anything more than some hot sex and some laughs.

This was a dumb stunt, and he shouldn't have agreed to be part of it. He still wasn't certain he shouldn't back out. But going for it would accomplish several things. He'd have something to do while he waited for his next race. He'd help the station, sort of a tip of his hat to his dad. And he'd get Jamie into his bed.

Okay, so he didn't give a damn about the station, and he'd never been bored a day in his life. The reason he'd said yes was that he wanted to sleep with the sex doctor. His motive wasn't so different from Darlene's—he wanted to show Jamie her theory was all wet.

He didn't listen to the radio often, but he did tune in to Jamie's show whenever he had the chance. He liked the sound of her voice, the way she laughed. In fact, after he'd seen her the first time, the talk show had taken on a whole new level of meaning. He'd never failed to get turned on by Dr. Jamie. Something about her stirred him up, made him hard. She was a fantasy, and soon she'd be a reality.

Jamie threw her headphones on the desk as the second commercial began. She didn't say a word as she yanked open the heavy door. A moment later Chase saw her approach Fred. Man, she was one angry lady. Of course, he couldn't hear the conversation, but he could read the expressions and the gestures. Jamie didn't want to play.

"I've got her," Darlene said, her voice barely above a whisper.

Chase wondered if she realized she'd spoken aloud. "What do you want her for?"

She jerked around to stare at him. "What?"

"You've got her. But what for? What's the point?"

"Come on. You see her. Love guru? She's barely out of her teens and she's become the expert on love in New York? I'm sorry, but that's bull. If she's an expert, then I'm the Queen of England."

"Maybe she's gifted. People are, you know."

"Gifted? I'll tell you how she's gifted. She doesn't get embarrassed about body parts. She has this sweet little voice, and this angelic little face, and she talks like a biology teacher on steroids. That doesn't mean she knows a thing about love or relationships. She's a fraud, and I'm going to prove it."

He nodded. "Nothing personal, though, right? Just doing the noble thing to protect the innocent ears of Manhattan youth?"

"Laugh if you want, but you know what? I am doing the noble thing. A fraud is a fraud is a fraud. She may look great on billboards, but she's a menace on the airwaves."

"And you're going to stop her?"

"Damn straight."

"What if it doesn't work? What if she doesn't fall for my charms?"

Darlene's eyes narrowed. "You won't let that happen. I know some things about you, Chase. You didn't say yes for me. You want to prove her wrong just as much as I do."

He shrugged. "Maybe. Which means I probably shouldn't do it. I don't have anything against Jamie."

"Come on, Chase. This kid is a flash in the pan. She's a marketing trick. She'll only be around until the next fad comes along."

The door behind them opened. Jamie walked in, her whole demeanor spelling out her defeat. This stunt could take her to the top, could make her a household name. And he held all the cards.

Chase wasn't crazy about that. She seemed like a nice kid. And damn, she was pretty. But what the hell? It was only radio. Just a stunt, like all the other stunts he'd pulled. In the long run, it didn't matter.

Despite what he'd said to Darlene, he would play fair. Of course, he'd use all the weapons in his arsenal. But if Jamie said no, it would stay no.

He knew he sounded like an arrogant bastard. But he didn't care about that. The truth was the truth. Women wanted to be appreciated; to be admired for who they were, not just what they looked like—although he didn't ignore that, either. Women wanted to be swept away. They wanted a man to run the show. They wanted to get well and truly laid.

What the hell. It was all just a game, right?

JAMIE HELD IT TOGETHER just long enough to finish the show. The moment she was off the air, she shot out of the booth and found Marcy and Fred in Fred's office.

She walked in and planted a fist on her hip. "I'm not doing this."

Marcy got to her feet, moving between her and Fred, a human blockade. "I'll handle this, Jamie."

"There's nothing to handle. I refuse."

"Ladies, take a seat."

Marcy sat, and once Jamie caught a glimpse of the expression on Fred's face, she sat down, too. It didn't mean she was going to budge.

"Do you have any idea how many people have called the station in the past hour? More than a thousand, and that's just the number we logged. Most people couldn't get through. I've gotten calls from the *Post* and the CBS affiliate, both of whom want to do stories on this."

"That doesn't make it right, Fred." Jamie leaned forward, putting her hands on his desk. "I won't subject myself to this kind of humiliation. No job is worth that."

"Really? That's surprising coming from you. Didn't you tell me last week you'd do anything to get national syndication?"

"I didn't mean it literally, for God's sake. Fred, the witch wants me to go out with that…that…man."

"That man is going to save your butt," Fred said. "You do know that his father built this station—that Chase himself could have owned the station, if he'd wanted to."

"So?"

"So you think he's going to let you fall on your fanny? The man is his father's son. He's going to do what's right."

Jamie slid back in her chair and crossed her arms over her chest. "Great. So not only am I going to be publicly humiliated, I'm going to do exactly what I've been accused of. It's called fraud, Fred, and they have laws about that.''

''All you have to do is not sleep with him. You said yourself, that was no problem.''

''That's exactly my point. Nothing can possibly happen. You know that, and I know that. Don't you see? It's not a contest. It's not even clever. It's just *that woman's* idea of clever.''

Behind her, a man cleared his throat, and she spun around to see Chase at the door.

''Sorry to butt in, but I figure I have a stake in this, so I might as well hear what's going on.''

''Come in, Chase.'' Fred waved him over to a straight-backed chair by his file cabinet, but Chase chose to sit in the leather wing chair by the bookcase. He sank down and opened the front of his jacket, revealing a plain, white T-shirt. His knees spread wide in that totally masculine, completely arrogant manner of men who think they're God's gift.

''I was just telling Jamie about your ties to the station.''

Chase nodded. Jamie didn't want to stare at him, but tearing her gaze away was proving a difficult task. Finally, she managed to turn in her seat so her back was to him.

''Hey, I don't care one way or another,'' Chase said. ''If she doesn't want to do this...''

''Jamie can't do this.'' Marcy stood up and walked to the file cabinet. Jamie noted that from there she could see all three of the players. ''It doesn't matter what that woman said. Jamie isn't a fraud. She has nothing to prove. Whittaker is just looking for cheap publicity.''

"And you're not?" Chase asked. "Isn't that the whole point?"

Fred nodded. "I can't force you to do this. But I'll tell you this—we have a chance at syndication without it. A chance. But if you do this thing—if you go out with Chase and keep your legs crossed—we'll be syndicated before the end of the year. Guaranteed."

"I don't want it that badly."

"Is that so?" Fred asked. "You're young and you have a brilliant career ahead of you. Why blow it over something like this? You play along for a couple of weeks, Chase says whatever he has to, and that's it. Except that we have a hell of a lot of new listeners. Believe me, it'll be worth it once we're national. The rest of your life depends on your decision here. You can make the best of it, or you can walk. Wasn't it you who told me you don't believe in half measures? That you were going to get syndicated before you were thirty if it killed you?"

"Wait a minute." Marcy shook her head as if she could hardly believe what was happening. "This is nuts. Why don't we all just think it through? Who says we have to decide right now? By tomorrow, things will be much clearer and—"

Jamie stopped listening. She had a decision to make. She could walk out now and not look back. She'd find another radio gig. She was number one in her market, for God's sake. On the other hand, what if Darlene was right? That she had no business telling New York, let alone the nation, a thing about life or love. It wasn't as if she hadn't wondered—as if her own doubts hadn't made her contemplate quitting. Did she have any right to help all those callers? Wasn't it only appropriate that she should be tested by her own fire?

She wouldn't sleep with him. No amount of charisma was going to change that. So why not go along with it? She loved this job. She wanted to be syndicated. She wanted to prove to herself and her family that she'd made the right choice. And lord, she didn't want Darlene to win.

She put up her hand, stopping Marcy mid-sentence. "All right."

"What?" Marcy headed back to her chair. "Jamie—"

"I said all right. I'll do it. But I'll only do it on the up-and-up." She turned her head so she could see Chase.

He looked at her with a curious smile. "You're sure about this?"

She nodded.

He stood. Walked slowly over to her. She almost bolted. With each step he took, her heart beat faster and her thoughts grew fuzzier. He was so big. So imposing. So unbelievably handsome. The truth was, he scared the hell out of her.

He stopped, but only when he was very, very close. He took her hand and pulled her gently to her feet. His fingers went to the bottom of her chin, and he lifted her face, forcing her to meet his gaze.

"Are you sure?"

She nodded, even though she wasn't sure at all—especially now that she could see his eyes. They were dark, mysterious, and they saw too much. That was it, of course. Why he frightened her. It was the way he looked at her, as if he could see all her secrets.

Still holding her chin, he leaned forward, and she understood what his intention was seconds before his lips touched hers. She didn't jerk away. She didn't push him back. She just closed her eyes.

Soft at first, teasing. His breath, coffee with a hint of peppermint. His size, imposing, almost threatening. But his lips were tender, even as the kiss deepened.

Somewhere out there, she heard Marcy's voice. Then the sound of her own heart beating drowned out even that.

Her lips parted, and he slipped inside her. Still soft. Achingly soft. He found her tongue and touched it, letting her taste him, igniting a tingle that spread through her like molten lava. Before the heat dissipated, he was gone. His tongue, his lips, his fingers. All gone.

She heard him chuckle, then she opened her eyes. He hadn't moved away.

"I'll give you tonight," he whispered so that only she could hear. "But tomorrow, you're mine."

"We, uh, need to discuss this," she said, surprised at how slurred her words sounded. As if she were drunk.

"We will. Tomorrow." His gaze roamed over her from face to breasts, then back again. "And put on your good underwear." He winked, then he was out Fred's door.

"Jamie?"

As she came out of her daze, the sounds of the room became clear again and she turned to Marcy. "Yes?"

"Honey, you don't need to do this."

"Yes, I do."

"He's dangerous."

"I know."

Marcy shook her head. "It's a mistake."

"Probably. But don't worry. I'm not helpless here.

I can take care of myself. You know, it's not all just talk. I do believe what I say on the air.''

''I know.''

Jamie smiled, although Marcy's doubt sat heavy in her chest. Who was she kidding? She knew books, not men. Definitely not men like Chase Newman.

She wasn't one to cuss. She'd always believed that if people tried, they could come up with better words, more exact words. But for the second time that night, all she could say was, ''Holy f—''

3

CHASE SETTLED more comfortably into the black
leather armchair and cradled the phone between his ear
and shoulder. Rupert Davidson, his business manager,
did like to talk. And talk. If Rupert wasn't so good
with money, Chase would have fired him years ago.
No, that wasn't true. Rupert had been part of his life
for too long. He had been his father's closest friend,
and he'd taken care of Chase and his mother after Jack
had died. What everyone except Rupert knew was that
he'd fallen in love with Chase's mother. Nothing would
be done about it until after a proper mourning period,
of course. Rupert would never disgrace Jack's memory.

Chase almost thought of Rupert as his stepfather,
which he could have been if he'd only asked. But his
mother couldn't or wouldn't urge him on, preferring
the romanticism of an unrequited lover to anything real.
It was an odd drama, played out over the years, one
which he'd learned to accept.

"...I want to roll the CDs over. I've done some in-
vestigation about GF Labs, and it's risky, but I think it
might be worth it—at least for a few hundred thousand."

"Do it." Chase looked at his coffee. It was on the
ebony-and-teak coffee table, out of his reach. He'd
have to move to get it, and he'd just gotten comfortable. So what was more important? The way the chair

molded perfectly to his back and shoulders? Or caffeine?

"Have you read the prospectus?"

"I don't need to. I have you."

"Dammit, son, don't you think it's time you accepted some of your responsibilities? Even one? You're thirty-one. You can't keep living like this forever."

Chase disagreed, but he didn't say so. He grabbed hold of the phone and leaned forward, bringing his coffee back with him. He tried to find the same position as before, but it was gone. He sipped the Kona blend, disappointed to find it was lukewarm. "Rupert, do we have to talk about this now? It's not even nine o'clock. I promise I'll call this afternoon, and we can fight all you want."

"I don't want to fight."

"Right. You just want me to do things your way."

"Not my way. The sensible way."

"Rupert, you're the most goddamn sensible man in New York."

"That's nothing to be ashamed of."

"I couldn't agree more." He liked Rupert, in his old-fashioned suits, with his antiquated sense of honor and obligation. He was refreshing, in an odd sort of way.

"How long are you here for this time?"

"A couple of weeks. Just till the racing season starts in Europe."

"You're going to see her, aren't you?"

"Yeah."

"And not just for an hour. She was hurt by that, Chase."

He closed his eyes, remembering the last visit with

his mother. He loved her, but sometimes it wasn't easy to like her. To say she wasn't thrilled with his lifestyle was an understatement. She wanted him to be like her, like his father. To get married, have some kids. She'd told him he embarrassed her. That he was disgracing his father's name.

"I'll try, Rupert."

"Don't try. Do it. She's the only mother you'll ever have."

"Okay, Yoda. I promise."

"Yoda?"

"Never mind. You go ahead and put my money where you think best. I trust you, Rupert. You've never steered me wrong."

"Thank you, Chase. But I'm not crazy about doing so much without your input."

"I know about fast cars and women, old man. You have a question about either one, I'm the guy you come to."

"Amusing. Very amusing."

"You take care, Rupert. And, for God's sake, propose to my mother already, would you?" Chase smiled as he heard the sputtering on the other end of the line. He decided to do Rupert a favor and hung up.

Cars and women. He'd said that last night, hadn't he? It was true. He'd put restrictions on his life just like his mother had put restrictions on hers. No wonder they clashed. They were too much alike.

He got up and went to the window. He liked to watch Manhattan wake up. His suite was on the top floor of the Four Seasons hotel, and he stayed here every time he came to New York. They knew him here, and they made sure he was comfortable. It was easier this way. Maids, room service, desk clerks. That's what he was used to. He had a place just like it at the George V in Paris, and another at the Chateau Marmont in L.A.

His gaze moved to the park. He loved it there, with all the kids on roller blades and the pigeons and the women with their strollers. Central Park always made him feel better, regardless of the season. Some of his favorite walks had been in the snow among the naked branches.

As he stared at the blanket of trees, ripe green at the height of summer, he thought about Jamie. He'd decided last night to call off the ridiculous stunt. He didn't need the aggravation, or the publicity. Sure Jamie was hot, but there were a million hot women in the city. He would call her today and tell her. She'd be relieved. He would be, too. Although, there was one thing he'd regret. He wanted to understand why he scared her so. Animals and children liked him. So what was she afraid of?

Such a paradox. The way she spoke was at complete odds with the way she looked. In fact, she was full of contradictions, and that certainly had its appeal. He enjoyed peeling back the layers. Not his own, mind you. But an interesting woman—that was something to be grateful for.

Those eyes of hers. One minute, radiating confidence enough to take on the world. The next, as frightened as those of a little mouse. Which was it? It occurred to him that he wanted to find out.

So okay, maybe he wouldn't call her. Maybe he'd go in person. She'd probably be up by now, right?

JAMIE STRUGGLED OUT of her dream and realized the banging she heard wasn't a demented jailor pounding on her cage, but someone knocking on her door. She glanced at the alarm clock on her nightstand. Eleven-fifteen. Odd, she never slept in. Her routine was to finish up her show at eleven, be home just after midnight, in bed by one, and then up at nine the next morning.

Another round of knocking spurred her out of bed. She padded across her wooden floor from the bedroom to the living room, then to the door with its five locks. Up on tiptoes, she looked through the peephole.

No one was there. That was weird. She undid each of the locks, poked her head outside the door. Nope. The hallway was empty. Had it been her nightmare? Her dream about being locked into something from which she couldn't escape had obvious connections to real life. She'd think about that later. Right now, her mind was on other urgent business. She closed the door and locked the dead bolt, then scurried to the bathroom.

Just as she was lifting her mouthwash to gargle, she heard the knocking again. She wiped her mouth with the back of her arm, then returned to the front door. This time when she looked through the peephole, the hallway wasn't empty.

Her heart thudded as she recognized the man standing at her door. Oh, God. What in heaven's name... He wasn't supposed to be here. She rocked back on her heels and ran her hand through her hair, which, thank you, made her look more like a porcupine than a person when she first got out of bed. To say nothing of her caked eye makeup, or the nightshirt that may have been snazzy back in 1994 but had gone straight downhill after that Laundromat incident in college.

She wouldn't answer. She didn't have to. He should

have called. Because there was no time to shower, let alone buy a new outfit.

He knocked again. Then just as she thought he was leaving, she heard voices and she cringed. What if he knew she was here? That she was completely undone by his presence?

She lifted herself to peephole level again. Mr. Wojewodka, the super, stood next to Chase. He had out his master key chain. The thing was monstrous, and when hooked, it pulled his belt and his pants down a good inch. Why was he searching through them now? Mr. Wojewodka was always harping on her to lock her doors, to carry pepper spray, to call him if she was ever in trouble. And now—

With a familiar squeal, the key entered the door. *He was letting Chase into her apartment!*

She'd never make it to the bedroom. Was the living room clean? No. Not important. Hiding was more important. Oh, God, the closest hiding place was the closet, and she made it there in two seconds flat. After a few more spent flailing about the knob, she pulled the door closed behind her. She forced herself to stand perfectly still, even though she was shaking with adrenaline, and listen as the two men entered her living room.

"She's a good kid," Wojewodka said in his thick Polish accent. "Gives me no trouble."

"Not even with her men friends?"

"What men friends? The girl is like a monk. She doesn't see anyone, except her crazy brother."

"Really?"

Jamie rested her forehead on the cool wood of the door as she plotted ways to kill her superintendent and Chase Newman. If she couldn't kill them, she'd sue their tails off. Talk about invasion of privacy! Or breaking and entering. Yeah. That was worse. But she didn't think they did any breaking. Just entering. Was entering against the law? Had to be.

"I really appreciate this, Max," Chase said. "I didn't like the idea of leaving this outside."

"I just hope she doesn't get mad at me."

"She won't."

Like hell. Jamie hadn't noticed Chase carrying anything. What was he leaving? She tried to see through the crack between the door and the frame, but that was useless. Maybe if she could get higher. She reached for the doorknob to get some balance, but even on tiptoes she couldn't see squat.

She gripped the knob with her hand as she flattened her feet, noticing something as she did so. A big, scary lump formed in her chest. The knob hadn't budged. She closed her eyes and said a short prayer, then she wiggled it. The knob didn't wiggle. It didn't do a damn thing.

Locked. How? Why? No, no, no. This wasn't funny. Wait. There had to be a way to unlock it, right? She ran her hand under the knob, over the wood, her movements growing faster as the repercussions hit her. *No, no, no, no.* This couldn't be happening. She'd be trapped. Better trapped than caught by Newman, though. The thought of how she'd look set her cheeks on fire.

Wait a minute. Maybe she should let him set her free. Then he'd have to explain what he was doing entering her apartment. But first, she'd have to explain what she was doing in her closet. Or would she? A person had a right to be in her own closet.

She lifted her hand to knock, then let it drop again.

"That's a big box," the super said.

"Yep."

"You gonna tell me what's in it?"

"Nope."

So Chase hadn't been putting on an act last night. He really did talk like Gary Cooper.

"I get it," Mr. Wojewodka said. "It's a surprise."

"Right."

Footsteps, followed by a *creak* of the front door. They were leaving. If she didn't do something now, she'd be locked in here for who knows how long—which would have been okay if only she hadn't decided to brush her teeth before taking care of her...other business in the bathroom this morning. Clenching her teeth and vowing revenge, she knocked on the closet door.

"Did you hear something?"

She didn't hear a response. Mr. Wojewodka must have shaken his head.

She knocked again, louder this time, cursing Chase, Darlene Whittaker, Fred Holt and everyone else connected to this malarky.

"Wait a minute." That was Chase's voice. "It's coming from the closet."

"Nah, couldn't be."

"Just hold on."

His boots sounded terribly loud on her floor. It was like listening to the firing squad take their positions. She wished like crazy that she'd at least had time to brush her hair.

He pulled on the door, unlocked it, pulled again—and this time the door swung open. She crossed her arms over her chest.

Chase looked at her with a completely calm face, as

if finding her in the closet was the most normal thing in the world. But after a few seconds his head tilted slightly to the right. "Are you trying to tell me you're gay?"

"No, I'm not." She stepped around him, making sure they didn't touch. Wondering if anyone had ever died of embarrassment. Perhaps she would be the first.

"I mean, if you are gay, that's all right."

"I'm not gay," she said, not daring to look at him.

"Ah. So actually being in the closet wasn't symbolic or anything."

"No. I was..." She cast about for an explanation, any explanation. "I was looking for my cat."

"You got a cat?" Mr. Wojewodka asked.

She whirled around to find the building superintendent at the front door. Great. A witness to her humiliation. It would be all over the building by rush hour.

"Did I say cat? I meant hat. I was looking for my hat."

Mr. Wojewodka looked at Chase. Chase looked back.

"Which," she said, raising her voice, "is completely beside the point. Care to tell me why you broke into my apartment?"

"I didn't." Chase nodded at Max. "He was nice enough to let me in."

She frowned. "Why on earth would he do that?"

"Because I didn't want to leave that outside."

She turned to where he pointed—to a long, gold box perched on her couch. Flowers. It had to be. Because what else would be in a flower box?

Quelling her urge to race over and rip off the top of the box, she faced Chase again. "Sometimes when a person doesn't answer the door, there's a reason."

"Right. I should have figured you were locked in the closet."

"I wasn't."

His right brow rose.

"It doesn't matter where I was, or what I was doing. My home should be private." She marched over to the door and Max, her bare feet slapping on the hard wood. "Mr. Wojewodka, I'm surprised at you."

He had the decency to look embarrassed as he leaned toward her. "Do you know who he is?"

"Yes, I do. Do *you?*"

"Yeah, sure. He's the top-seeded race-car driver in America. In the world."

"And this makes him able to enter any apartment he wishes?"

"He was your friend. I did him a favor."

"He's not my friend."

"Right," Chase agreed. "I'm just supposed to seduce her. That's all."

Jamie winced. "About that..."

Chase moved over to the couch. It was a normal couch, but when he sat down it looked very small. She'd gotten it at an estate sale four years ago, along with the matching wing chair. She'd had them reupholstered in a cheery floral print, which Chase's presence also changed. She'd never realized the material was so feminine.

"About last night—" she continued.

"You don't have to apologize."

"What? I wasn't going to."

"Oh, okay." He smiled at her, and his teeth were slightly crooked, which for some reason made him even sexier. His eyes were perfect and so was his hair and his chest. The fact that his nose was a little crooked didn't detract from his face. On the contrary, like the small flaw of his teeth, it made him look more ruggedly handsome than if it had been straight.

"What do you mean, apologize?"

"Nothing. It doesn't matter."

"Yes, it does."

"I just figured, with you being in that bind and with me volunteering to help you out…"

"I wasn't the one who asked you to play this game. That was Whittaker, remember?"

He nodded. "She would have done it, you know."

"Done what?"

"She would have smeared your reputation, made sure there was plenty of bad press about you. She doesn't much care for you."

Jamie's hands fell to her sides. "Why? I never did anything to her."

"Don't tell me you don't get it. You're too smart to play dumb."

"Oh, you think she hates me because I'm successful? Because people listen to me?"

"That. And the other."

She wasn't about to ask what he meant. This whole conversation was going poorly, and the smart thing to do would be to stop right here, right now, and get Chase and his number-one fan the hell out of here.

She put her hands on her hips and opened her mouth to tell him to leave, but before the words came out, his gaze moved from her face to her chest. As he blatantly stared, his face changed. He smiled. Devilish, wicked, hungry. She felt her nipples harden and poke at her flimsy T-shirt.

"You're beautiful," he said, his voice low and seductive.

She turned away, crossing her arms once more. "Please leave. And take the box with you."

Max stepped outside the door, leaving her with Chase. She wanted him gone, too, even as his compliment swirled inside her head. He thought she was beautiful. It wasn't that she saw herself as ugly...but beautiful? That wasn't what mattered about her. She was smart, and she was ambitious, and she was able to talk to people. She'd never gone after beauty. Oh, she'd had compliments before, but as her mother was so fond of saying, beauty was the shallow refuge of incompetence.

He came up behind her, and her heart beat so hard she thought it might burst. When his hand touched her shoulder, her knees weakened and she forgot how to breathe.

It was nuts. Crazy. Why was she feeling like this? Chase was just a man. No big deal.

He turned her around until she faced him. Her arms were still covering her breasts, but from the way he looked at her, it was too little, too late. He'd seen her reaction. She closed her eyes.

"Jamie."

She shook her head. "Please, go."

"Jamie, look at me."

She didn't want to. But she couldn't help it. Her eyes opened to find him closer still, close enough for her to see the gold in his dark brown eyes.

"I was going to call it off," he whispered. "Then I started thinking about you. By the time I got here, I'd changed my mind."

"Why?"

He smiled, and her tummy got tight with a wave of desire. "There's something about you."

"What?"

He shook his head. "I don't know yet. I'll tell you when I find out."

"You don't have to. The hell with Whittaker and her magazine. I don't care what she says about me."

"Neither do I. But I do want to spend the next two weeks getting to know you, magazine or no magazine."

"I don't see why. You're a big-shot racing guy. You date movie stars. You live a different kind of life than me. Frankly, I'd bore you silly."

"You let me be the judge of that."

"What if I don't want to see you?"

He leaned forward until their lips almost touched, pausing for an instant, and then he captured her lower lip between his front teeth. A second later, he let her go, only to steal her breath with a kiss, his soft lips on hers, his tongue teasing her mouth open. Her eyes fluttered closed and her arms moved from her chest to his back. With gentle pressure, he rubbed his chest against hers, sweeping against her nipples. Pleasure and heat flowed from her breasts down to her stomach, and then lower still. She squeezed her thigh muscles, but the feeling didn't go away.

He did something terribly wicked with his tongue, thrusting it inside her, then pulling back, as if showing her what he wanted to do to her body. Goose bumps covered her flesh as vivid pictures came to mind. Him, naked—oh lordy—thrusting into her, making her scream.

She whimpered. He moved his lips from her mouth to her ear. "I'm going to explore every inch of you, Jamie," he whispered, his hot breath making her shiver. "I'm going to know you better than you know yourself. And I'm going to give you pleasure you've never even dreamed of.''

Then he stepped away, and, before she could catch her breath, she heard the front door close.

When she got it together enough to walk, she went to the couch and took off the top of the gold box. Two dozen red roses were flared beautifully, the long stems stripped of any thorns. She picked up the small card lying to the side of the flowers: "Dear Jamie, I dreamed about us. You had roses. See you tonight, Chase.''

She picked up the box and brought it to her face so she could smell the flowers. His scent lingered, despite the sweet aroma of the gift. She could still feel his hard chest, his big hands, his soft, talented mouth.

Oh boy. She was in trouble. Bad trouble. She headed for the kitchen and a vase. Her first flowers, ever. And they were from a man who was from a completely foreign world, a man with enough experience to host his own radio sex show.

She put the box on the counter and stared out her window. The view from here sucked. It was just another building. And when she looked down, all she saw was a walkway where no one ever walked.

She couldn't let him into her life, not even for a moment. He was dangerous. He did scary things to her body. To her mind. Given even the slightest opportunity, he'd find out. Even if he never touched her down there, he'd know. He'd see it in her eyes, feel it when she trembled in his arms. And if he found out—the rest of the world would find out, and where would she be then?

No one had ever given her roses before. Because no one had ever been close enough before. She'd been busy with school, with the radio show. She'd never dreamed things would happen so quickly for her, or so publicly. But they had, and here she was.

Whittaker was right. She was a fraud. The honorable thing to do would be to quit. But that would kill her. She'd never loved anything the way she loved her show, loved its callers. And she knew she was helping. Honestly.

There was just the one problem, the one that could ruin everything if it ever got out. The fact that she was, at the ripe old age of twenty-six, a virgin.

4

JAMIE GOT to the station a little after five-thirty. Determined not to dig herself in deeper, she had spent the day trying to figure out a way to extricate herself from this mess without ending up fired. Unfortunately, all the ideas she'd come up with so far required either some form of magic or breaking several major laws.

She stopped at the reception desk, where the night guy, Geoffrey, smiled broadly as he gathered her mail. Over six foot five and thin as a rail, the twenty-year-old had neon-orange hair and more piercings than her aunt Emma's pin cushion. The pierced body parts were offset, of course, by tattoos ranging from the sublime (a perfect, tiny red heart at the base of his neck) to the ridiculous (Bart Simpson, bent over, pants down, eyes drawn on the buttocks).

She shifted her briefcase to her left hand as she took the unusually large stack of mail. "Thanks."

"My pleasure."

His tone made her pause. So did his grin, which had widened dangerously, exposing the braces on his molars.

"What?"

"Nothing." He arched his right brow. "Except that the switchboard has been lit up all day. I swear, girlfriend, Mr. Holt has a major woody over this little stunt of yours. Brilliant." He crossed his arms over his Amazon.com T-shirt and idly fingered his nipple ring through the material. "And excuse the hell out of me, but could Chase Newman be more divine? I don't think so."

"Why don't *you* go out with him?"

He sighed. "If only."

She shook her head as she headed toward her office. File cabinets on both walls made the hallway narrow, and if someone had to find a file, all traffic came to a halt. Oddly enough, in her time here she'd only seen a file drawer open once or twice. She imagined they were filled with old ad logs and personnel files.

It wasn't until she neared her door that she heard her name from across the way. Elliot Wolf, the program manager, waved at her while he talked on the phone. Jamie sighed. Like the Energizer bunny, this nightmare kept on going and going and going....

"Sit," Elliot said, then to whomever was on the phone he added, "Tonight at the Palm II. *Ciao*."

She didn't want to sit. She didn't want to talk. She was cranky and getting crankier by the minute.

"So," he said, running a hand through his Brad Pitt hair, complete with dark roots. However, the likeness ended there. From the forehead down, Elliot looked eerily like a young Vincent Price, mustache and all. On the gaunt side, with a voice a little too high, he devoured scary movies like Raisinets, and his hobby, like Vincent's, was gourmet cooking.

"Elliot, I have work to do."

"I know. This'll just take a minute. Sit."

She obeyed, giving him a pained sigh in protest. She hated the chairs in his office. Leather and chrome, they tilted back, making it hard to get out of them again. But they looked chic, and Elliot loved chic. He'd decorated modern, with a very expensive, very ugly Chuck Close print dominating the room. He never had anything on his desk but his notebook computer, as clutter was one of his pet peeves. He had no such qualms about his secretary's desk.

"Here's the scoop." Elliot perched on the edge of the credenza. "We're running highlights of your shows for the next two weeks. Sound bites the other DJs will play before commercials. I'm working with Cujo on the reels. We've set up a separate phone line for people to call in their comments and suggestions. Holt is planning a major ad campaign, which means we need you and Newman for photos. Greg Gorman is going to do the shoot, but he only has two hours on Tuesday available, so if you have something scheduled at eleven, cancel it."

Jamie sat perfectly still, afraid that if she moved she'd throw up all over his Berber rug.

Either Elliot didn't see her distress or he chose to ignore it. "We've already heard from Independence. They love it. They want it. And dammit, Jamie, you'd better sweep Newman off his goddamn feet. I'm not kidding. We need this to happen."

With her education and résumé, she felt reasonably sure she could get a job at McDonald's. Because she certainly wasn't going to be working in radio much longer. What really got to her was that yesterday her world had been nothing but roses. Now, all she had were thorns.

"Why aren't you smiling?"

"There's nothing to smile about. I can't do this, Elliot. I mean it."

His pale face grew paler. "Don't do this to me, Jamie."

"I'm not doing it to you. I'm not doing it because it's a terrible idea. There's no way in hell I'm going to let Chase, or any other man, seduce me. Not in two weeks or a hundred. So what's the point?"

"Publicity." He leaned forward, putting his hands together as if in prayer. "This is the best thing that's happened to this station since I came on board. Don't you get it? We all win with this. You get syndicated, I get a monster raise, Fred gets to be the big hero, and Marcy can name her own price."

Jamie couldn't look at the desperation in his eyes. "I never signed up for this. My personal life should be my own."

He leaned back. "In a perfect world. But, honey, this is radio. And opportunities like this don't fall in your lap very often."

She grunted. "Opportunities. Right."

"It is an opportunity. If you use it. You're smart, now be savvy. Milk this baby until it's dry."

"Is that it?"

He nodded. "Don't forget about Tuesday."

She hoisted herself out of the chair and headed toward his door. She stopped there, facing him head on. "No. You have pictures of me. I'll play along, but I won't help." She left the office.

"Jamie..."

She just kept walking.

CHASE LOCKED UP his bike, grabbed his helmet and walked into the radio station. It was almost eleven, and Jamie was nearly done with her show.

He wanted to see her. Except for racing, little excited him these days. Not even other women. One was much like another, and while his libido was always fully engaged, his interest rarely went beyond the bed. Jamie was interesting. He'd thought a lot about why, and the only thing he could come up with was that she wasn't at all what she appeared to be.

His last "girlfriend," for want of a more accurate description, had been exceptionally beautiful. A model, in fact, who had surprised him with her intelligence and curiosity. But for two weeks he'd watched her primp in front of any mirror she could find, anguish over the right dress, pour all of her energy onto the pages of *Vogue*. She'd wept when he'd said goodbye, but she'd made sure her mascara hadn't run.

Jamie was probably more of the same. Not that she was obsessed with her looks, though he felt pretty certain she was obsessed with her work. But, hell, this was only going to last a couple of weeks, and she did present a challenge.

He wanted to see what she'd do. And he wanted to sleep with her.

He'd tried a lot of things in his life, almost everything at least once. He wasn't into games, or sex that required a bunch of props. But something about Jamie made him want to pull out all the stops. That innocent act of hers fired him up. What would it be like to tie her to the bedpost and make love to her until she begged for mercy? That image had plagued him all day. Of course, he'd have to work up to that. She wasn't about to give in without a fight.

The receptionist's eyes widened as he walked into the office, but Chase was used to that. As celebrities went, he wasn't a real contender, but he did get great seats in restaurants and theaters, along with the occasional rabid fan. He smiled at the young man. He didn't get the whole piercing thing, though. What was the point? But to each his own.

"Mr. Newman."

"Chase."

The smile the young man flashed turned flirtatious. Chase wasn't interested personally, but like piercings, the flirting didn't bother him.

"She's got about ten minutes left of her show."

"Thanks. I'll just go on back." He headed down the hallway, and, as always, the ghost of his father floated on the walls, in the sound his boots made on the thin carpet. Chase tried hard not to remember too much. Not because the memories were painful but because they made him feel weak. He missed his father. He missed the sound of his voice, the way he looked in his dark suits.

A publicity poster of Jamie brought him back to the present. He studied her for a moment. Mostly her eyes. They were so damn big, almond shaped, framed with thick, dark lashes. Her nose, in comparison, was small, but her lips…ah, man, they were great. Just right. Plush and smooth… He hurried past the poster toward the booth.

He stopped at the production booth first. Cujo waved him in. Chase liked him, even though the guy was strange as hell—maybe because of it. Cujo was the ultimate techno-geek. His long blond hair was always unkempt, his chin most times in need of a shave. He lived in jeans and Metallica T-shirts, and he loved his job almost as much as he loved to smoke a joint at the end of the night.

"*Uno momento.*" Cujo toggled some dimmers on the board, bringing up a commercial for cell phones. "How you doin', bro?"

Chase shook his hand. "Hanging in."

"That's what counts." Cujo nodded toward the broadcast booth. "You be careful in there. She's a mite prickly."

"Oh?"

"She told a caller to quit jerking off."

"And that's not her usual modus operandi?"

"Jamie? Hell, no. She believes everyone is worth saving. Man, she should meet a few of my friends. That'd change her tune."

Chase turned toward the window. Jamie sat behind the desk like the captain of a spaceship, her controls at her fingertips, the great, fuzzy mike inches from her mouth. She'd seen him. She didn't appear overjoyed. In fact, her scowl seemed downright unfriendly.

It was show time.

"What did Jon say this morning?" Jamie said into the mike, ignoring Chase with due diligence, even when he sat down and put on his own set of headphones.

"He said he forgot that we had a date," said the caller. "He's the one that wanted to go out tonight."

Jamie turned a quarter of an inch in her chair. Away from him. "Gabby, we've talked about this before. Jon has a habit of forgetting dates."

"But why?"

"I don't know. But I do know you can't keep doing this."

"Doing what?"

"Depending on Jon for your happiness. Gabby, do you honestly believe he has your best interest at heart?"

Jamie shot Chase a quick glance. He leaned back in his chair, put his feet up on Jamie's desk and clamped his hands behind his neck. He closed his eyes, listening to Jamie's voice, letting his imagination run full throttle.

"But, Dr. Jamie, he said he loved me," Gabby said. She plucked another tissue from the box on the coffee table and wiped her eyes. Usually, Dr. Jamie understood. In the past few months, she'd been about the only one who understood.

"Does he show you?"

"Sure."

"How?"

"Well, he tells me I'm pretty and he likes my hair."

"I didn't ask if he told you he loved you. I asked if he shows you."

"I don't understand."

"That's right. I don't think you do. What matters is how he treats you, Gabby. If he puts your feelings ahead of his own. If he respects you and honors you, and he shows you kindness."

"He does."

"Does he?"

Gabby looked at the phone, then put it back to her ear. "Well, not all the time. But no one could do that."

"You don't think so?" Dr. Jamie sounded a little upset. "Tell me something, Gabby. Do you wait all day for Jon to call? For him to come over? Does life begin when he's there and fade when he's not?"

"Well, sure." Gabby looked over at the dining room table. She'd paid almost five dollars for the flowers in her mother's favorite vase. And she'd put out the company china. She'd bought him the knife he'd been looking at in his magazine, and she'd wrapped it real pretty with the bow-making machine she'd picked up at a garage sale two months ago. As of four o'clock this afternoon they'd been going together for two years. She remembered their first date like a photograph. Everything about it had been perfect. Her dress. His smile. The way he'd kissed her. But lately he hadn't seemed real excited to see her, not like in the beginning.

"I think that's a problem, Gabby. We'll talk more about it after the commercial."

Gabby heard the music that meant Dr. Jamie had to do something during the break. Sometimes they chatted, just like real friends. But most times, Gabby went on hold. She suspected, although she'd never ask, that Dr. Jamie had to run to the little girls' room. She couldn't very well stop her show to do her business, could she?

Gabby had made Jon's favorite meal. Lamb chops. She'd even found the little booties that slipped over the bones. In the beginning, he'd gone on and on about what a good cook she was. He hadn't said that in a long time. Of course, they hardly ate any meals together. He was so busy at work. If he kept on going like this, he'd make himself sick.

She sniffed again, dabbed her eyes with her tissue.

"Gabby?"

"I'm here."

"Do you think it's fair that Jon should have to be responsible for your happiness?"

"He's not responsible. But I love him so much that when he's here, I'm happy."

"What would his reaction be if he called you for a date, but you were busy doing something that makes you feel good? That gives you pleasure? Something yours and yours alone?"

"Well, I don't know. I don't think he'd be very happy about it."

"I think he'd be relieved, Gabby, that you were taking care of yourself. That he didn't have to come up with some way to make your day. That the pressure was off him."

"It's not pressure to want your boyfriend to come home to his anniversary dinner."

"I know, Gabby. You're hurt and frustrated. When you talk to him, try to tell him what happened, but tell him in a way that doesn't blame him. Just talk about how you feel."

"I feel terrible."

"It'll get better. It would get better faster, though, if you'd go to counseling."

Gabby sniffed again. "I'll try."

"Okay. Thanks for calling."

"Bye."

The line went dead, and Gabby dropped the phone into her lap. The tears that had been under control while she'd talked to Dr. Jamie poured out now. Rivers of hurt, oceans of disappointment.

The dinner was ruined, and so was her life.

"WE'RE BACK, and we have time for one more caller." Jamie pressed line four, Audrey from Teaneck, who wanted to talk about Chase. Everyone, except for Gabby, poor thing, wanted to talk about Chase. About the bet. About seduction.

Obviously, Chase thought it was highly amusing.

He'd shown up just when she'd thought she was safe. And during the last commercial break, he'd told her he'd made dinner reservations.

"Um, hi, Dr. Jamie. Is, um, Chase there?"

He leaned in to the mike, all the while staring at her, smiling as if he had a secret, and, boy, was she going to find out what it was.

"I'm here."

"Hi, Chase. My husband thinks you're a shoe-in for the Budapest race."

"Thank him for me, although nothing's for sure."

"No? Then you think you won't be able to seduce Dr. Jamie?"

He laughed, and the sound rippled through Jamie. The last thing on earth she wanted was to be turned on by Chase Newman. Unfortunately, her body wasn't getting the urgency of her message. When he looked at her, she went all smooshy inside. Oh, great. Now, she was losing her mind. A *cum laude* PhD didn't use words like *smooshy*.

"I think it's going to be a hell of an interesting ride finding out."

"Me, too. We've got a pool started at the office. My money's on you."

"Why?"

"Because I've seen your picture. Honey, if I wasn't married…"

Jamie leaned in to her mike. "Now, come on, this isn't funny. Women have to take responsibility for every part of their lives."

"I know," Audrey said, "but I also think you're not accounting for sex appeal."

"I am. But I'm also accounting for reason. For judgment. For prioritizing. Women have to stop letting men make their decisions for them. We're not the weaker sex."

"I completely agree," Chase said. "You're not the

weaker sex. In fact, you're strong as steel. But you also need a little romance.''

"Romance and seduction are two different things.''

"Not if you do it right.''

"That might be true for the women you've gone out with. But, in my book, a woman doesn't let honeyed words and flattery alter the facts of a relationship. As I was saying to Gabby, it's the actions that count, not the flowers, not the compliments.''

"Uh, Dr. Jamie?''

"Yes?'' Damn, she'd forgotten Audrey was on the line.

"What are you going to do tonight?''

She looked at Chase. He winked at her, which thoroughly ticked her off. But she couldn't afford to tell him to leave. Not yet. "We're going to dinner.''

"Where?''

"I don't think it's a good idea to say.'' Jamie cleared her throat. "We do need a certain amount of privacy.''

"Besides,'' Chase said, "I didn't tell her.''

"It sounds like you have the whole night planned,'' said Audrey.

"I do.''

"You think tonight will be the night?''

"I hope so.''

Jamie took a calming breath. This conversation was not going well. "It will not.''

"Dr. Jamie? Is he as gorgeous as his pictures?''

Jamie closed her eyes. "He's very nice looking.''

"My friend Ellen said he has a butt to die for.''

"I wouldn't know.''

"I don't mean to be rude, Dr. Jamie, but with an attitude like that, you'll win this bet hands down...but it won't be fair.''

"Thank you, Audrey. I'll take that under advisement. This is Dr. Jamie on WXNT. Ted Kagan is up next. Speak to you tomorrow."

She clicked off her board and swung around to face Chase. "You're getting a kick out of this, aren't you."

He nodded.

"Tell me. Is it the fact that I'm being humiliated, the fact that you're getting your own little fan club, or both?"

"Both."

"Wonderful."

Ted opened the door, his hands full of files for his show. Jamie nodded curtly and stowed all her gear to make room for him. Chase lifted the bundle of papers and articles out of her arms. It was such a courtly gesture.

"Jamie, honey," Ted said, "you need to move your behind."

She jumped out of the way, then led Chase to the door. As she reached for the handle, he again stepped in and did it for her.

"Are there things you have to do before we go?"

She thought about telling him she wasn't interested in dinner, but that would be a lie. She'd thought about what Elliot had said. The game was on, and she needed to be a savvy player. "I have to speak to Marcy and put my things in my office."

"Lead on, McDuff."

Marcy was in the production booth. She'd pinned her hair up, which made her neck look long and elegant. Her outfit added to the image, the dress hugged her curves but not too tightly. Everything about her looked polished. Jamie knew Marcy was putting on the dog for Ted, but she didn't think Marcy was aware of it.

"Great show." Marcy smiled at Chase. "And thank you for coming by. I wasn't sure you would."

"I almost didn't."

Jamie looked up. "What changed your mind?"

He met her gaze. "You."

"I don't understand."

He nodded. "My point exactly."

The all-too-familiar heat came to her cheeks and, needing something to do, she took her things from his hands. His response shouldn't have surprised her. He was following a typical male pattern—trying to disarm her, charm her. And the whole eye-contact business was right out of her textbooks. Eye contact was the first stage of the mating process, the first real evidence of interest.

What she didn't understand was why she was falling for it. This was a game to Chase, he was only here out of boredom. And yet, her insides fairly quivered when their eyes met.

"Jamie?" Marcy's brows had furrowed. "Are you all right?"

"Yeah, sure."

"I was saying that it would be great if you two figured out what you were going to do over the weekend. And I'd like you to call in. I'll figure out times tonight."

Jamie nodded, but inside her panic light had gone on. What was she going to do with him over the weekend? It couldn't be anything too private. The safest way to keep her secret intact was to avoid any situations that could lead to intimacy.

Chase took Marcy's hand and kissed the back. It

could have been creepy, but it wasn't. It made Marcy giggle, which hardly ever happened. She even futzed with her hair. The man had the touch. Oh man, did he have the touch.

The hole Jamie had dug for herself suddenly got a lot deeper. Damn, damn, damn.

CHASE WATCHED her fingers as she toyed with her spoon. She'd ordered tiramisu but so far she hadn't tasted it. Or her cappuccino. If she'd eaten four bites of her dinner, he'd be surprised. She was scared. And he was a bastard for enjoying it.

"I'd planned on going into private practice, but all that changed when I did the radio show at the university."

"You fell in love."

One side of her mouth quirked up. "I suppose you could say that."

"It's a good thing. Passion is important."

"What are you passionate about?"

"Racing."

"Why?"

He shifted in his chair and looked around for the waiter. "I like the speed."

"And the danger?"

He nodded. "Yeah."

"Have you always been an excitement junkie?"

"Pretty much."

"The need for adrenaline can be quite compelling. I read a study about people who need danger in their lives. The theory is it's chemical… What?"

"Where did you come from?"

"Huh?"

"Where were you born?"

"Minnesota."

"Brothers, sisters?"

"One brother, Kyle. He's a neurosurgeon at Cedar Sinai in L.A."

"Are your parents in the medical field?"

She nodded. "They're both gynecologists."

"That explains a lot."

"What do you mean?"

He shook his head. "Did they help you get through school so fast?"

"No. Well, maybe some of it had to do with my family. Mostly, I just liked school. I was good at it."

"I'll bet you were. When all the other kids were out getting sick on beer and pizza, you were in the dorm, studying the night away."

"Well, yes. I developed good habits early. I'm not ashamed of it."

"I wish I'd known you in college."

"Why?"

"I would have taught you a few things."

"What, like taking drugs or drinking? No, thanks."

He shook his head. "Nope. My curriculum would have been a whole lot more personal than that."

She cleared her throat and turned her spoon over. "My education was quite well rounded, I assure you."

"Uh-huh."

"So what about you? Your parents? Your education?"

"My mother lives here in New York. She's very busy."

"And your father?"

"He died when he was thirty-five."

Sympathy changed her face. On most people, that look of sorrow and empathy would have been bull, but something told him Jamie wasn't shoveling. Of course, that's what made her good at her job. She cared about people. Or else she was a master at pretending.

"I'm sorry."

"Me, too." He caught the waiter's attention and asked for the check. Turning back, he nodded toward her dessert. "You going to eat that?"

"Oh." She took a bite. "It's good. Would you like some?"

He took her spoon from her fingers and brought it to his lips. He licked the remnants of her bite, tasting her along with the sweet concoction. She blushed again, which was the point.

JAMIE WISHED it wasn't so humid, but she couldn't expect anything else in August. The rich folks were ensconced in the Hamptons by now, leaving the rest of the population to sweat it out. Still, this was her favorite time to be walking. Well after midnight, the streets weren't so crowded, the smells of the city weren't too overwhelming. And the Fifth Avenue windows were all still lit; the expensive trinkets and high-fashion clothes seemed like a private exhibition for her benefit alone.

Of course, her attention wasn't completely on the displays. They'd walked two blocks now, and at the corner of 44th and State, Chase had put his hand on the small of her back.

She'd tried to get him to talk about himself. That was one of her surest techniques. Most men found themselves utterly fascinating. But Chase kept bringing the subject back to her.

He leaned down, his lips close to her ear. "Tell me a secret."

The shiver went all the way down to her toes. ''Pardon?''

''Tell me something you've never told another living soul. Something wicked.''

''You go first.''

He laughed, a deep, rumbling sound that swirled around her like a mist. ''All right. When I was fourteen, I drove a car for the first time.''

''That's wicked?''

''Considering it was a stolen limousine, yeah.''

''You're kidding.''

''Nope. It was a big old stretch limo. Belonged to my father. I decided I wanted to go for a ride. And ride I did.''

''What happened?''

''They eventually got it out of the swimming pool, but the car never was the same after that.''

She laughed, and it felt wonderful. For the first time since she'd agreed to this farce, she felt relaxed. Thank goodness for humor. She said that a lot on her show.

As her smile faded, her focus returned to his hand, which couldn't possibly be as hot as it felt. The warmth came from her mind, her imagination. Whatever caused it, the sensation intensified by degrees, and without giving him any warning, she stopped at a window. It was just a drugstore, and the displays were mostly paper goods, but it did the trick. Her back was Chase-free. And cold.

He came to her side. ''Low on paper towels, are you?''

''No.''

''Then, why did you stop?''

She shrugged. ''It's getting late.''

He touched her. ''Come on.''

She walked with him again. Just as it had warmed her back, his hand simmered on her arm. They didn't speak, but she felt him, felt his presence in a way that was new and scary as hell.

They turned a corner, and Chase moved closer to her. Something shifted, as if the air had become electrified. As if she'd forgotten how to breathe. He moved his hand to the back of her upper arm, guiding her steps, moving her away from the curb. Away from safety. From sanity.

His grip tightened, his pace quickened, and the next thing she knew, he'd pulled her into an alley. It was very dark, and she couldn't see his face. Fear jackhammered in her chest, and she tried to pull away. He pushed her against the wall, the brick rough on her back. He took her hands in his and pushed them against the rough wall, too, on either side of her head. The concrete scraped her flesh.

She couldn't escape, and she didn't understand, and her heart beat so fast and hard she wasn't sure she could take it. But something else was pulsing, too. Her breasts, and lower still.

The scent of baking bread snuck in between the dank smells of the alley, but when Chase pressed against her, it was his scent that took over. Masculine, slightly spicy, with a hint of sweat that made her insides clench.

He stole away her breath as he captured her lips. His kiss was as hard as the wall behind her, as hot as her flesh where he touched her, as scary as the dark recesses of the alley. His tongue thrust in her over and over, and his mouth widened and narrowed as he ravished her.

No one had kissed her like this before. It was a new thing, unique in its power to make her tremble. He invaded her mouth, took liberties with his tongue. Intimate, like sex itself, and she felt helpless to stop him.

And then his hips moved against hers with deliberate intent. He wanted to stir her into a frenzy, and, God help her, he was succeeding.

He pulled back, took his lips away, and she couldn't stop the tiny moan of disappointment. The only thing she could see was the outline of his head, his unruly hair. Not his eyes, though. She knew what she would have seen there—lust, and just a hint of cruelty.

"This is the first night," he whispered. "Before it's over, I'm going to have you in my bed. There are things I'm going to do to you. Things that will scare you, that will make your heart beat the way it is right now."

"No." She tried to push him away, but his hips ground into hers, keeping her still.

"I see the truth in your eyes. That untamed part of you is in there, and it's starving to death. I'm not going to let that happen. I didn't agree to this stunt because I was bored. I agreed because you wanted me to. Because you knew I wouldn't stop until I'd had you."

"I didn't—"

"Don't worry. I'm not going to take you against your will. I'm not even going to try to convince you. I'm going to wait until you beg me."

"I won't."

He let go of her right hand and cupped her between her legs, the intimacy shocking her. "You're on fire already," he said. "And we haven't even begun."

She closed her eyes, turned her head to the side, not willing to look at him even in the darkness. Because she *was* on fire.

CHASE LET HER GO for all the wrong reasons. Touching her was meant to shock her. He hadn't been prepared for a jolt of his own. It was all he could do not to take her, right here, right now.

He didn't like this. Not a bit. He never lost control. Not in a race, not with a woman. He steered the course—alone. He wasn't blind to his need to be in charge. It was all about power, and the illusion that the world didn't give one damn about him or his plans.

But with this one—this slip of a girl—something was going wrong. When he'd kissed her, it was bad enough. The taste of her, the way her shy tongue finally touched his, threatened his control in a way he'd never imagined. He felt almost…helpless.

And then when he'd touched her, felt her heat, imagined her naked up against that concrete wall in the middle of the city as he thrust into her over and over—

She gasped, and he realized he'd leaned forward again, his erection straining for release, pressing against her body as if she'd let him in.

"Chase," she murmured, her voice soft and trembling. "Please."

"See what you do to me?" he said, lowering his lips to the shell of her ear. "You want this as much as I do."

"No."

"Liar."

She didn't take the bait. Her chest rose and fell against his, her breasts teasing him to the edge of his endurance. And then she moved her head, slowly, until her lips brushed his. He tasted her breath as she whispered, "No."

5

"WELL?"

Jamie didn't look up. Instead, she studied the commercial lineup for the evening as if it were a matter of life and death.

"I can wait here as long as you can. Longer. I don't have a show in ten minutes."

Jamie raised one brow, then let her gaze follow. "We had dinner."

"Where?"

"A restaurant."

"Ha, ha."

"Marcy, I don't want to talk about it. The whole thing is one big charade, and I'm counting the seconds until it's over."

"So something did happen last night."

Jamie gripped her papers tighter so her hands couldn't get to Marcy's throat. "Nothing happened. It was dinner. We chatted. We walked. He went home. I went home. The end."

"He didn't make a move on you?"

Jamie looked at her papers again, trying to find where she'd left off. "No."

"Liar."

"Hey."

"Honey, I took a lot of cockamamy courses at NYU.

One of them was on body language. And you are not telling me the truth.''

"Okay. Fine. Have it your way. He kissed me."

"That's better." Marcy slid her right hip onto Jamie's desk and leaned forward. "Details, please."

"There are no details. He kissed me. And he said he wouldn't do anything I didn't want him to."

Marcy leaned back and gave her a quick once-over. "Is that why you're dressed like somebody's aunt Fanny?"

"I'm not." She looked down at her dress. It was a little on the baggy side, but so what?

"And I suppose it's a coincidence that you didn't have time to put on makeup. Or do something with your hair?"

"I happen to think I look fine this way."

"You lie like a rug. You're putting up defenses, my friend. And the only reason to put up defenses is because you think he's got a shot."

"A shot at what? Seduction? Please, Marcy, do you think I'd abandon my beliefs so easily?"

Marcy shrugged. "Personally, I don't think he can seduce you—but not because of your beliefs. I've thought a lot about you, Dr. Jamie, and your lack of male companionship."

Jamie's heart thudded in her chest. "I've been busy."

"Or scared."

"Marcy, we haven't known each other long enough for you to make such an assumption."

"Maybe not. But I'll tell you my theory, anyway. I think you were hurt badly—probably in college, but maybe high school—by someone you loved a great deal. And I think you're scared to care again because you think it was maybe your fault.''

Jamie started to tell Marcy that she was way off, but she swallowed her rebuttal in a muffled sort of grunt.

''I knew it.'' Marcy stood and smoothed down her already smooth, gray slacks. ''You're not the only relationship maven at this station.''

Jamie nodded. ''I don't like to talk about it. I hope you understand.''

Marcy's victory smile faded. ''Of course. Oh, hon, I'm sorry. I didn't realize.''

The lie lodged in her chest, right next to her heart, making it hard to breath. She gathered her papers together. ''It's all right.''

Marcy didn't stop her as she left the office and headed for the booth. Thank God. She couldn't have kept up the charade for another second.

This was just swell. A whole new layer of torture. She hated lying, and she was terrible at it. But Marcy's explanation was so much better than the truth. In fact, that story was probably going to save both their jobs. She'd have to refine it, give it the details that made a story believable...and stick to it until the day she died.

She pushed open the booth door, relieved that Chase wasn't there. He hadn't spoken to her since last night. In fact, he'd left her right after the incident in the alley.

The thought conjured the image of his body pressed against hers—and her armload of paperwork fell all over the floor. She bent to gather her things, remembering the heat of his erection, the strength in his hands. The confusion when he'd led her from the alley, hailed a cab, put her in the back seat and closed the door. The yearning to take back her ''no'' and make it a ''maybe.'' She hadn't gathered her wits until long after he'd paid the driver. In fact, she wondered if she'd ever have her wits about her again.

"Anybody home?"

Jamie grabbed the last newspaper clipping and stood up to find Fred Holt standing just inside the door. "Hello, Fred."

"Hello, my beauty. I have a surprise for you."

She groaned inwardly. Just a few days ago, his announcement would have filled her with anticipation. Today, dread washed over her like a bucket of cold water. "What now?"

"What now? Jamie, you're the talk of the town." He stepped closer and threw a folded newspaper on the empty desk. She recognized immediately that it was the *Post*, arguably the most notorious paper in New York.

"Go ahead." He nodded. "Check out the headline."

All things considered, she'd rather not. It couldn't be good, not with the way her luck had turned.

Fred couldn't wait any longer. He retrieved the paper himself and opened it so they could both see the over-size type of the headline.

The Sexpert And The Playboy!
Will He Seduce Her? Or Will She Just Say No!

She read with mounting horror that in offices all across Manhattan, bets were being wagered, sports pools formed, sides taken. Someone claiming to be an ex-lover of Chase's was quoted as saying Jamie didn't stand a chance: Chase could seduce any woman in any country in any language. He'd leave Jamie broken and heartsick as he sailed off to his next race.

But that wasn't the worst of it. Somehow, they'd

gotten hold of Dianna Poplar, one of her college room-mates. Dianna and she hadn't known each other well, mostly because Dianna had majored in sex, drugs and rock-and-roll. But now, Jamie read that Dianna "...had been like her sister." Dianna said Jamie was so smart and clever, but she didn't date much. The inference was that perhaps Jamie didn't have to worry about being seduced by Chase because she was more interested in someone like Dianna.

Jamie wobbled over to her chair and sat down.

"Isn't it great?" Fred kept holding up the paper as if she was next to him. "You're a household name. Everyone in the city is talking about you. *People* magazine called. So did *Cosmo*. This is brilliant. We're all gonna be rich."

If reporters had gotten to Dianna, they could get to other people who'd known Jamie in college—people who'd tell the world that she'd been a bookworm and a social outcast. That she'd never had one single date, let alone a lover. Maybe it wouldn't be so terrible to have the world think she was gay. At least she'd have had some experience. Her cover was going to be blown any second, and the potential for humiliation was expanding exponentially.

Fred closed the paper. "What's wrong?"

"Oh, nothing."

"That's good. We wouldn't want anything spoiling this. It's our ticket, Jamie. Our big hairy multimillion-dollar ticket."

"Right."

"You're on the air in two minutes."

She nodded, tried to put her papers in some kind of order, even though she couldn't focus. When she looked up, Fred was gone, Cujo was giving her the count, and in five, four, three, two—

"This is Dr. Jamie Hampton. And we're talking about sex."

MARCY TYPED IN the information for the tenth caller, then turned the phones over to Alexis, one of the new interns. Jamie didn't sound too good. Who could blame her? It was lousy that she'd been caught up in this, but that was radio for you. Marcy had been involved in a lot of stunts in her day, but this one was the craziest. But she'd bet the farm that it was going to be the most lucrative stunt she'd ever seen. She was due for national syndication. She'd been in radio for eighteen years, working her way up the slippery ladder. Jamie was her ticket.

Jamie was also her friend. And Marcy had a feeling this wasn't a completely awful thing for her. Jamie needed to get out there, to live life instead of just talking about it on the airwaves.

Chase wasn't a complete unknown, although he was at most an acquaintance. What she did know about him made her feel secure that he wouldn't hurt Jamie—not in the traditional sense, at least. He was a heartbreaker, there was no denying that—but this was only for two weeks, and surely nothing that terrible could happen so quickly.

She just hoped Chase would prime the pump for Jamie. Let her see that she could risk her heart again. Poor thing. Her college sweetheart really must have done a number on her.

But then, who hadn't had a sweetheart that did a number? She'd had hers—a charming, devilishly handsome man who'd stolen her heart at the age of twenty-two. She'd leaped into the marriage bed, only to realize her husband already had a lover—scotch. For six tumultuous years she'd hung on to his falling star, but she'd had to leave before he hit bottom. She simply wasn't able to take it.

Marcy chased away her memories, walked over to the window and focused on the show.

JAMIE PUT DOWN her empty teacup and concentrated on her caller's question. "Can you be a little more specific?"

"Yeah," Bev from Lincoln Heights said in her thick New York accent. "I'm just, you know, curious about this G-spot thing. Is that for real? My boyfriend—he said it was a bunch of bull."

"Oh, it's real. First, so you know, it was named after Dr. Ernst Grafenburg, a German gynecologist, who discovered it. The G-spot is about two inches along the inner upper wall of the vagina between the back of the pubic bone and the front of the cervix. There's a bundle of nerve endings there that may be more sensitive than the rest of the vagina. Although, this isn't true for all women. But it's worth exploring."

"Uh, how?"

"Have your boyfriend insert his finger inside you, palm facing up. When he's in all the way, have him rub the flat of his fingertip in a "come here" motion. You'll know right away if your G-spot is sensitive."

"What's supposed to happen?"

"Nothing's *supposed* to happen. But you may feel stronger sensations and climax sooner. So I suggest you go for it."

Bev laughed a little, which was normal. In fact, the

whole conversation had been normal. Jamie relaxed as she finished off her tea.

"Did *you* go for it?" Bev asked.

"Pardon me?"

"Does Chase Newman know where your G-spot is?"

The second his name was out there, Jamie's body filled with heat. It wasn't embarrassment and it wasn't arousal, but it was something real close to both. "Not from personal experience, no."

"So what happened on your date?"

"We talked," Jamie said, trying to keep the anxiety from her voice. "We found out a few things about each other."

"What'd you find out?"

Think, Jamie. What had he said? "Um, he doesn't have a house. He lives in hotels."

"Cool. Why?"

"Because he travels so much."

"So did you go back to his hotel?"

"No, I didn't. Get your mind out of the gutter, missy."

Bev laughed. "But he's so gorgeous."

"Be that as it may, sex is not something that's going to happen. Not by accident or by design. No seduction, remember?"

"Yeah. Well, when is he coming back to the show?"

"I don't know. But I do know it's time for us to take a break. This is Dr. Jamie, and we're talking about sex."

She took off her headphones, pressed the mute button and leaned back in her chair. "The Sexpert and the Playboy?" God, she'd never live that down. The name would stick with her and make it virtually impossible for anyone in her field to take her seriously. A private practice would be a joke. Marvelous. She'd lose her radio show if anyone found out the truth, and now she didn't even have a backup plan. Maybe she could be a waitress. They made pretty decent money.

"Hey, kiddo."

She looked up as Marcy's voice came over the intercom. "Yeah?"

"You okay?"

"No."

"Can I do anything to help?"

"Shoot me."

"Other than that?"

Jamie shook her head. "No, wait. Tea. I have no tea."

"Coming right up. And Jamie?"

"Huh?"

"Cheer up. It's just radio. No big deal."

"Uh-huh."

Marcy gave her a perky little thumbs-up before she headed out the production booth door. Jamie let her head drop, and it hit her desk with a resounding *thunk*.

"Ow," she whispered. Was it possible to feel worse than this? To be more screwed? Wait. It wasn't smart to think that way. The gods always knew when she figured she was at bottom, and then they opened up a trap door.

The last thing she needed was a new low. Maybe Chase had grown bored with her. She'd expected him to be here. To discombobulate her with his slow smiles and his heat. She should be thankful, right? Only, she wasn't so much thankful as disappointed. Which made her certifiable. Completely whacko.

"Jamie?"

She lifted her head from the desk.

Cujo smiled at her from the other room. "We're almost on."

She adjusted her headphones, and pasted a smile on her face. Just then, Ted and Marcy walked into the production booth. Ted had his hand on the small of her back. Marcy was laughing about something. Then Ted moved away and Marcy turned to the window. She waggled here eyebrows and mouthed, *Oh my God!*

Jamie's smile became real, and, a second later, she was on the line with Ellen from Old Westbury.

"I've got one for you, Dr. Jamie."

"Shoot."

"What's the difference between a golf ball and a G-spot?"

"What?"

"A man will spend half an hour looking for a golf ball."

Jamie laughed. "Ellen, that was great. Just what I needed. Thank you."

"Sure thing, Dr. Jamie. Oh, and one more thing."

"Yes?"

"When you see Chase, give him a big old kiss from me, okay?"

Jamie shook her head. This Chase business wasn't going away. She was cursed. Cursed!

THE SOUND of her footsteps brought him out of his meditation. He'd learned the Zen practice years ago from a Tibetan monk he'd met in Italy. At first he'd just meditated before a race to clear his mind, but slowly the ritual had become a habit, and he always made time in his day for the deep relaxation.

But tonight's session, attempted while leaning

against Jamie's door, hadn't been relaxing at all. Jamie
had seen to that. No matter how hard he'd tried to clear
her image from his mind, she'd lingered. Her full lips,
the way her skin felt under his palm, her wide, almond-
shaped eyes. He'd actually become aroused, and that
was one hell of a surprise because in his thoughts she
was fully clothed.

"What in the world?"

He looked up. She stood a few feet from him, her
arms loaded down with a grocery bag and her purse.
He'd surprised her, and that made those eyes of hers
widen so that she reminded him of those *anime* car-
toons. Hoisting himself up, he took a moment to appreciate the rest of her face. Especially her lips. He
liked them parted like that, ripe and ready for kissing.

"What are you doing here?"

"Waiting for you." He lifted the grocery bag from
her arms. "What did you buy?"

"Dinner." She added, "For myself."

He looked at the vegetables, the small package of
chicken breasts. "I can make it stretch."

She blinked at him for a moment, then got her key
out of her purse. Once she'd opened the door, he
slipped inside quickly, not giving her a chance to tell
him to leave. From there, he went right to her kitchen.
It was small, but then this was Manhattan. Only the
rich or those in rent-controlled apartments had the luxury of space.

"Excuse me, but I don't recall inviting you to dinner."

"That's okay. I like to cook. Maybe you could open
a bottle of wine or something."

"But—"

He put down the groceries and opened the fridge

while she sputtered. It was cute sputtering, and he resisted the smile that tugged at his lips.

"Are you listening to me?" she demanded.

He spied a bottle of chardonnay and pulled that out. Then he opened cupboards until he found the wineglasses. "Here," he said, handing them to her. "Do you have any linguini?"

She nodded. "In the cupboard. Hey, wait a minute."

He crossed the kitchen and opened the pantry door. The linguini was on the top shelf, and so was the olive oil. He took both. Only when he was at the stove did he turn to Jamie. "Yes?"

"I want you to stop this. I'm not a child. This is my apartment, and I say who comes in here."

He walked slowly over to her, plucked the bottle and the glasses from her fingers and put them on the counter. "I'm sorry," he whispered as he pulled her into his arms. "Can you ever forgive me?"

He bent down, gently brushing his lips with hers, amazed once more how the slightest touch made him a little bit crazy. He licked her lips, tasting her on the outside before he dipped inside and tasted her there, too. The hell with dinner. He would dine on Jamie, until he'd sampled every inch. Then he'd go back for seconds.

She tried to push him away, but only for a moment. Once the kiss deepened, she surrendered. In fact, she sort of went limp on him. He took her hands and wrapped them around his neck. She got the hint and splayed her fingers, massaging him just enough to make his eyes close. He left her lips, but only to bring his mouth to her ear. "Say it tonight, Jamie. Say you want me."

The whispered entreaty didn't have the desired ef-

fect. She let go of his neck and stepped away, turning
so her back was to him. "I'm tired."

"All the more reason for me to make you dinner.
You're in charge of the wine, and then you have to
step aside. I need some elbow room."

She faced him again wearing a cynical frown. "Oh,
please."

"What? You don't think I can cook?"

"I think you know how to make spaghetti. You
don't even have a house, and the last I heard the Four
Seasons doesn't have kitchens in the suites."

He didn't answer her. The food would be the proof.
He got busy, first with a pot of water to boil, then with
making the sauce. The wine forgotten, Jamie watched
him. He focused on the preparations, using the knife
like an old friend. He'd learned his skills years ago
from a French chef. She'd schooled him in many techniques, not the least of which was how to please a
woman with his lips and his tongue. Jamie would get
the full benefit of his education. Tonight, she would eat
well. And later tonight? If he had anything to do with
it, she would learn his other secrets firsthand.

When the vegetables were ready, he pulled out another pot and put it on the stove. Still, he didn't look
at her. Not until the last of the spices had been added
to the gently simmering sauce. When he finally turned
to her, she blushed. Her cheeks turned a soft pink and
she wouldn't meet his gaze. Her thoughts hadn't been
on pasta. But what had she been thinking? Had she
wondered what his hands would be like on her flesh?
How he'd treat her like the rarest delicacy?

He approached her slowly, not wishing to scare her
off. She stepped back, but she didn't bolt. An extraor-
dinary beauty, she did her best to disguise herself. But

her baggy clothes weren't disguise enough. He knew what lay beneath—the gentle curve of her waist, the slight roundness of her belly...

Reaching up, he touched her chin with the length of his finger and raised her head. Her gaze darted away, but he wasn't in any rush.

Finally, she looked right at him. The blush on her cheeks deepened.

"What are you afraid of?"

She didn't answer, although her mouth opened slightly as if she wanted to tell him.

"It's all right. You can tell me."

"There's nothing to tell."

"No?"

She looked away again.

He moved closer to her, close enough that the hem of her dress brushed his jeans. "Just to set your mind at ease, I do know."

"Know what?

"Where your G-spot is. Among other mysterious female secrets."

Her gaze snapped back. "You listened?"

"I did. And I hate to say it, but I don't think you're trying very hard."

"Please don't tell me you're taking this seriously."

He nodded. "Of course I am."

"I already said it wouldn't happen."

"That's it, then? You're not even going to give it a chance? See what could happen between us?"

She moved away, grabbing the wine bottle as she crossed the kitchen. "Your water's boiling."

He turned to the stove, but not before his gaze was caught by a vase filled with his roses. They were on her coffee table, and they still looked as fresh as they had when he'd brought them. He smiled, then added the pasta to the water. After that, he stirred the sauce and adjusted the flame. She was at the counter struggling with the cork.

He could have taken it from her, but he didn't. Instead, he watched her try to yank out the cork. She didn't have the right leverage, which made the task twice as difficult as it could have been.

She was a stubborn little thing, though, and despite her stance, she succeeded, and the cork popped loudly in the small room. He brought her the glasses, and she poured his glass and her own, but hers she filled to the rim.

His guess was that she figured the liquor would calm her nerves. Doubtful. But it would loosen her up a bit, and for that he was grateful.

She was a puzzle, this one. He tried to think of a woman like her and he came up blank. She was a beauty who behaved as if she wasn't. A sophisticate who blushed at the first hint of impropriety. There had to be a key to Jamie. A clue that would make all the pieces fit.

He couldn't imagine a more entertaining project.

"Jamie?"

"Hmm?"

"You've told me a lot about your past, but not enough, not nearly enough..."

"I've already told you everything that's important. I really have a boring little life."

"I don't believe that for a moment." He sipped his wine, then leaned back against the counter and made himself comfortable.

"It's true." She picked up the big wooden spoon and stirred the pasta, then the sauce.

''No sale. Come on. I want to hear about all the men in your life.''

She picked up her wineglass, brought it to her lips and drank—didn't sip—until half the glass was gone.

His brows lifted. He'd pitched and scored. All this mystery was about a man. Was he in her past, or in her present?

''Excuse me.'' Jamie put her glass down and headed toward the hallway.

He watched her until she'd entered the bathroom and closed the door. Interesting. Of course, he'd figured it was something along those lines that made her so shy.

Now, all he had to do was find out what the man who broke her heart was like, and be the opposite. Piece of cake.

6

JAMIE PUT DOWN THE LID and sat on the toilet. "Oh God," she whispered. It sounded good so she said it again and again until it was one long word. *OhGodOhGodOhGod...* What was she supposed to do now?

Maybe if she sat in here long enough, he'd go home. Even as she thought it, she knew it wasn't going to happen. Chase wasn't the type to tiptoe out the door. He was in her face, and he wanted answers.

She hadn't had time to make up her past. Her ex-lover didn't even have a name yet. Steve? Frank? Buddy? Alonzo? Her head dropped to her hands and she moaned, the small bathroom bouncing the sound right back at her. She sounded pitiful. She *was* pitiful.

The fact was, she had two weeks to get through, and she'd better get a grip or she was going to lose it, big time.

What if she'd called herself for advice? What would she say?

First, she'd ask herself if she was out of her mind for getting into such a ridiculous situation. But then, she'd probably ask what she wanted the outcome to be. Did she, in fact, want to win this bet or did some part of her want to be seduced by Chase?

Okay. Point one—she wanted to win, and not just because she didn't want her secret blown. She wanted to get closer to her listeners. She wanted them to trust her and feel comfortable asking her the most intimate questions. She wanted to help women see their part in the seduction scenario.

Then she'd ask herself if she was doing everything she could to win the bet. That would be a big no. In fact, she hadn't taken the initiative once. She'd let herself be buffeted about like a leaf in a gale. Every time he touched her, her resolve weakened a notch. He'd kept her off guard, which was how things got out of hand.

Point two—it was time to go on the offensive.

So then she'd ask about the, uh, situation. The one where she'd lose everything she cared about if the truth were to get out that she was indeed the phoniest of the phonies. That she knew about sex like fish knew about bicycles. However, she'd remind herself, the whole point of the game was to avoid being compromised, so what the heck was the problem?

Could she keep saying no to him? Yes. Of course. How ludicrous. No way she was going to succumb. Even though, oh God, she kinda sorta wanted to.

The confession made her moan. How was this possible? The bet, although embarrassing, should have been a no-brainer. She didn't believe in seduction, and therefore it wasn't going to happen.

But when he kissed her... She moaned again as her traitorous body reacted to the thought. "Reacted" was putting it mildly. Just thinking about his mouth on hers put every nerve ending in every erogenous zone on full alert.

Tough. It wasn't going to happen, couldn't happen, so she'd better get used to it. According to everything she knew about sexual intimacy, kissing didn't happen right away. Lots of things happened before getting that close. Eye contact. Light touches. Mirroring behavior. Asking the right questions. And sex? Please. That was the last step. She knew the road, which meant she didn't have to walk down it, right? She counseled a lot of women to watch for the signs, to keep one step ahead. She'd simply take her own advice.

Point three—no woman can be seduced. Period. No ifs, ands or buts. If she didn't make eye contact, or touch him, or mirror his behavior or ask intimate questions, she'd be fine. Because no amount of sexual chemistry was equal to the power of self-determination. She was stronger than her hormones. She was stronger than Chase. He didn't stand a chance. So what was she worried about?

A soft rap on the door made her jump.

"Jamie? You okay?"

"I'm fine," she said, trying to sound normal as her heart pounded in her chest.

"Okay. Just thought I'd tell you dinner is ready."

"Great. That's...that's great. I'll be right there."

Silence as the seconds ticked by. "All right," he said finally.

She rolled her eyes. *Way to take charge, Jamie.* Next time, she must remember to call Dr. Ruth.

MARCY FOUND an empty booth at the back of the diner. It wasn't the most elegant of restaurants, but it served good food at decent prices, and they were open until two in the morning. She'd been coming here for several years, and not just because of the food or the fact that it was across the street from the station. She never felt awkward here eating alone. No one bothered her. She

could read as she ate, sometimes the paper, sometimes
a novel. It was nice, quiet and safe.

She grabbed a menu, but before she could open it
she heard Jamie's voice. Surprised, she looked up, then
realized she was listening to the radio behind the
counter. Fred was running lots of clips through all the
programs. A "Best of..." series.

"What are you so afraid of?" Jamie asked.

"I don't know," came a soft response.

"What's the worst thing that could happen?"

"He'll laugh at me."

"And?"

"I'll be humiliated."

"Have you ever been humiliated before?"

A sigh. "Yes."

"Did you survive?"

"Yeah."

"So, in other words, if you ask him to sit with you
at lunch, he can say yes, he can say no, or he can laugh
at you. Now, the odds are that third thing won't happen. But let's say he says no. What would that mean?"

"That he doesn't like me?"

"Maybe. Or maybe it means he has other plans for
lunch."

"Oh."

"Or maybe it means he's seeing someone else, and
because he finds you attractive it wouldn't be a good
idea to sit with you at lunch. Or maybe it means he's
gay. Or he's got crabs. Or a hundred other things, none
of which have anything to do with you."

"Okay. I get it."

"Do you?" Jamie asked. "Do you see that fear is
stopping it all? Stopping your life? That you'll survive
even if it is awful, and, more than that, you'll have

pride in yourself for taking a chance, for risking your heart. So, you go for it, girl. You ask him to eat lunch with you. He might just say yes.''

''That was Dr. Jamie, and she talks about sex weeknights…''

Marcy tuned out Barry Leland's voice. He was on the air now and probably irritated as hell that he had to promote Jamie's show.

She looked at the familiar menu and decided to stick with her usual Santa Fe chicken salad. She really should try something new, but not tonight. Not with the blue funk that had her wrapped in its fuzzy arms.

It wasn't that anything was wrong so much as that not much was right. Dee, who worked here six nights a week and almost always waited on Marcy, came over and smiled as she got out her order pad. ''Santa Fe salad, right?''

Marcy nodded. God, she was so predictable.

''Iced tea?''

''No. I'd like a beer. Whatever you have on tap.''

''You got it.'' Dee finished writing, then stuck the pencil behind her ear. Her hair was so short, it was almost a buzz cut, but on her, it worked. ''That's something about Dr. Jamie, huh?''

''Yes. It is…something.''

''I've seen that guy. He's a tall drink of water. I sure as hell wouldn't kick him out of bed for eating crackers, if you know what I mean.''

Marcy grinned. ''I do indeed.''

''Not that he'd want an old broad like me.''

''You're not so old.''

Dee shrugged. ''Going on fifty. But it beats the hell out of the alternative, eh?''

''You bet.''

The waitress headed toward the kitchen, and Marcy's gaze went to the door as a man walked in— only it wasn't just any man, it was Ted. Her pulse kicked up and her cheeks heated. She'd invite him to sit with her. He was a co-worker, right? People ate with co-workers.

She smiled as he looked her way. He smiled back, but then he turned to a woman behind him. A beautiful blonde with arched eyebrows and pale pink lips. Ted touched her upper arm, leading her to a table. A table far too close to Marcy's. What was he doing here so late?

Something broke inside her. A last hope, perhaps? She had no idea who the blonde was. But by the way Ted touched her, Marcy guessed she wasn't his kid sister.

There was no reason for her chest to hurt. For her appetite to disappear. For a wave of sadness to make her want to cry. Ted wasn't her boyfriend. He didn't even know she was interested in him. Why? Because she was a big, fat chicken.

What was it Jamie had said? Fear can stop it all. Is that what her life was about? Hiding from fear?

Her answer came a few minutes later when Dee brought her salad. A lifetime of Santa Fe salad when there was a banquet being served? Is that all she was worth?

She looked over at Ted's table. He glanced her way and smiled. Only she didn't do the usual blush-and-turn. This time, she held his gaze. Just held it with her own.

He didn't turn away. On the contrary, his right brow lifted a hair, and his smile changed from an impersonal greeting to a question.

Marcy's heart beat so fast that she hardly remembered how to breathe. Finally, after what seemed like forever, she lowered her lashes and broke the connection.

She managed to shove a few bites of food into her mouth while she tried to get a grip. Eye contact. She'd heard Jamie talk about it again and again, but she never dreamed it could work.

One more bite, then she dared another look. Ted's gaze met her own, and there it was again. A connection. A silent Q-and-A session. A moment.

He was the one to turn away this time. But he didn't want to. She could tell. *He didn't want to.* This was major. This was unbelievable.

"Thanks, Jamie," she whispered. "I owe you."

HE'D FOUND HER CANDLES. She kept a basket by the bookshelf in the living room where she stashed an eclectic collection of candles, from beeswax to scented votives. Most had been given to her as gifts, a few she'd bought herself, but she'd never placed them all over the dining room, and she'd never turned off the lights and lit them all at once.

It didn't feel like her apartment. It didn't smell like her apartment, either. The scent of Italian spices made her tummy growl. The scent of the candles made her giddy. The scent of Chase Newman did several other things, none of which she cared to focus on.

Chase stood between the kitchen and the dining room. He'd also found her place mats and silver, and the table looked sinfully elegant. Candles, of course, were the centerpiece.

"Welcome back."

"You did all this."

He nodded. "I had some time on my hands."

"Sorry."

"It's all right." He headed toward her, lit by soft, flickering lights. "Are you?"

"Am I?"

"All right?"

"I don't know," she said, which wasn't smart. But she couldn't help it. Her pep talk in the bathroom was fading like a bad dream.

"My linguini will fix everything," he said, his voice low and intimate as he held out her wineglass. "But first, you need to relax."

"I'm fine," she said, lying through her clenched teeth. She took the wine, thinking it might be a good idea to drink as much as she could as fast as she could.

He had other plans. Starting with a walk around her, a steadying hand keeping her from moving. Once he was behind her, he put his hands on her shoulders. She nearly dropped her glass.

His hands covered most of her shoulders, they were so large. The first wave of sensation was all about her own size, her fragility. How it would feel to have those hands caress her body. A shiver raced through her, and then he started massaging her, kneading her neck muscles.

He was surprisingly gentle. His thumbs found her pressure points, and she could feel herself melting. As if his magic fingers weren't enough, his warm breath whispered against her neck—her name, so soft it was hardly there. Then his lips were behind her ear, nuzzling as he continued working the tension from her body.

This was all new to her. No one had ever touched her exactly like this, or whispered her name in such a way. His shivery kisses made her want to weep for all she'd missed out on.

She'd thought it would be wonderful. Honestly, she'd fantasized about a man like Chase, a moment like this. But her fantasies had been woefully inadequate. No imagining could equal the feel of his hands running down her arms, the erotic web he wove with his breath, his lips, his hips rubbing against her bottom.

He slipped her wineglass from her hand and put it somewhere. She'd forgotten all about it. Her intoxication didn't need liquor, it seemed. Just Chase nibbling on her earlobe.

It wasn't fair. All these new sensations, and she couldn't let herself enjoy them. Well, not as much as if she were really going to make love with him. This was all about a bet, a wager, a game. He wasn't touching her this way because he wanted *her*. If it hadn't been for Darlene Whittaker, Chase wouldn't have asked her out in the first place. She must remember that...

His hands moved down her arms again, and then they were on her stomach, and she gasped when he didn't stop there. He moved his hands up just under her breasts, and then his thumbs, those wicked thumbs, rubbed her just below her nipples.

A hiss of breath hit her neck, and she had to squeeze her legs together tightly. She put her hands on his hands, meaning to pull them away, but then she seemed to lose her strength, to say nothing of her determination.

He teased her, but only until she whimpered. Then his thumbs touched the rigid nubs. Rubbed small circles, not too hard, just right. Behind her, he moved his hips, letting her feel his hard length straining against his jeans. That was new, too. She knew so much about men in general, and so little about a man.

He cupped her breasts, so small in his big hands. But his moan let her know he liked what he felt, that she was right for him.

"Jamie," he whispered. Then he turned her around and his lips came down on hers.

The kiss was different, hungrier. His tongue thrust between her teeth, taking all he wanted, his hands on her back and then lower until he cupped her buttocks and pulled her tight against his heat.

She wasn't equipped to fight a man like Chase. He was too sophisticated, too devilishly handsome. His hands...they could make her do anything. The fact that he didn't really want her so much as he wanted to win the bet couldn't compete with the way his taste, his lips, his hands squeezing her flesh made her woozy with desire.

It would be her job. Her career. Unless she could convince him to keep her secret. But either way, she just couldn't fight him any longer. He'd won on day two. A TKO of the first magnitude.

She broke the kiss, raised her gaze to his.

He didn't seem surprised. He smiled, making her heart flutter. But then he did something that changed the whole game. He chuckled. It was very soft, and if she hadn't been watching him so intently, she would have missed it.

He'd known exactly what would happen. That with a touch here, a word there, he could make her melt. He was almost right. Almost.

She still tingled from head to toe. Her nipples were still hard and the throbbing between her legs was enough to make her yearn for release. But there was just enough sanity left in her to see what was happening. To understand that she was in the game—whether as a pawn or a queen was up to her.

The easiest thing in the world would be to surrender. To let go of her ideals and blame biology. But surrendering wasn't her style. She'd fought hard and long for everything she had in her life. Including her job. Her place in the world.

Was she going to lose it all to this cocky bastard?

"What's that smile for?" he asked, his voice gruff with the lust she still felt in his hands, in his body.

She moved her hands down his chest, brushing lightly with her fingertips. *Come on, girl. You know how to do this.* She knew how to exploit a situation for her own benefit. Hadn't she done that with the radio show? With school? Of course she had. So why couldn't she do the same thing with Chase. Turn the tables. Be the seductor instead of the seductee. She could hold all the cards, every last one. And Chase wouldn't know what hit him.

Her fingers moved down to his belt where she lingered for a moment, teasing the buckle as if she were going to undo it. His breath caught. She gave him a suggestively raised brow. Then she purposely stepped away.

Wait for it… Wait… There.

He let out a frustrated moan, chalking one up for her side.

Take that, Chuckles.

HE'D HAD HER. So what the hell just happened? A moment ago she'd been putty in his hands.

"Did you say dinner was ready?"

He nodded. Watched her get her wine, take a sip,

smile at him over the rim of the glass as if she knew a secret. Then she walked to the table, running one hand down her backside, showing him the shape of the curves he'd only begun to discover for himself.

The real problem here was physical. It wasn't the first time he'd been left dangling, so to speak, but it hadn't happened for years. Women didn't turn him down. Not women he went after in high gear.

The feel of her hard nipples, the way she fit into his hands...

What the hell—?

"Chase? Would you like me to serve you?"

"Sure." As long as it was her on a platter. The pasta held no appeal. Nothing did, except finishing what he'd started.

She busied herself with the plates, gave them both generous portions, but she didn't dig in. Instead, she ran the tip of her finger over the rim of her nearly empty wineglass and looked at him from under her dark lashes.

She was coming on to him, right? The fingers, the glances, the subtle smile, the flush in her cheeks. She wanted him. But if that was the case, why was he over here, and why did she have her clothes on?

"It smells wonderful. I was wrong. You do know how to cook. I should have guessed."

He needed to move. To go sit down. To pick up where he'd left off. Only, something was screwy.

He understood women, almost as well as he understood cars. They were predictable in their unpredictability. They wanted to succumb, to be swept away. When Jamie had leaned back in his arms it had told him everything he needed to know. Only, he had on his clothes, too.

"I'll be right back." He took an uncomfortable walk to the bathroom and shut the door behind him. Once he was alone, he leaned against the wall and willed himself to calm the hell down. The pressure eased a bit, which let him think more clearly.

Okay, so maybe Jamie wasn't the pushover he'd imagined. Maybe she'd take a little more work. Which made sense. Hell, look what she did for a living. He'd figured she wasn't very experienced. A hundred small things told him that. The way she blushed, her tentative kisses, the way she trembled in his arms. All signs of a woman who hadn't had any in a while.

He'd been with women like her before. Shy women who'd had inadequate lovers, who ate up the attention and longed to be set free.

But none of them had stopped midway through the first lap. Certainly not after they'd found his belt. Dammit, that was usually a sure sign.

He splashed some cold water on his face as he tried to assess the situation. There was only one pertinent question—did he honestly believe he could seduce Jamie? Could he shake her down from her intellectual pedestal? Could he make her surrender?

Yes.

Why?

Because of the wager? No. It was a stupid bet, and the only intelligent thing to do was bow out. He knew without a doubt, though, that if he called off the bet, he'd lose his only hope of getting her into bed. She'd run and hide, just the way she used to at the station before all this started. He used to wonder why he frightened her, and the last couple of days had shown him why.

So the bottom line was simple. Screw the bet, and

get Jamie Hampton into his bed. That was the game. That was the goal. Like winning at Le Mans.

He looked at his reflection. Why not? What else did he have to do that was anywhere close to this fascinating? Good for her, knocking him off balance. That made things…interesting.

Dammit, he wanted to win.

What was the expression? *Live hard, die young, leave a good-looking corpse?* Hell of a motto, but then he didn't have much choice in the matter, did he? After all, he had the Newman curse.

That was his ultimate strength—the knowledge that he'd only be around for a few more years. No one else knew, and he wouldn't say a word. He'd just go at thirty-five, as had his father and his father before him.

The doctor he'd talked to said it was a coincidence, but the doctor didn't know about Chase's great-grandfather. Dead at thirty-four. A heart attack, out of the blue. His mother knew, and in those first years after his father died, she'd warned him not to repeat his father's mistake. Not ever to leave a wife and child behind.

At least Chase had some warning. And he'd taken it seriously. He did live fast, as fast as he knew how. He'd been all over the world, been with women from Africa to Istanbul. He'd tried everything at least once, daring himself to go farther, deeper, and to risk more. And he'd never let anyone get too close.

His mother had nearly gone insane at the death of his father. No way would Chase leave behind a grieving widow, or a son who would have to face the same destiny.

He lived for the moment, never for the future, never in the past. And, right now, his moment was in the dining room. If she wanted to roll up her sleeves and fight, so be it. In fact, he liked that she wasn't going to be easy. Too damn much in his life had been.

He had no doubt he'd win. But now, getting there was going to be a lot more fun.

Grabbing a towel from the rack, he wiped his face and hands, then headed back to the dining room. At the far corner of the table sat Dr. Jamie, his worthy opponent. Her dark eyes flashed with a seductive welcome.

But he had her number. Oh, yeah. *Baby, the flag is up.*

7

JAMIE WATCHED HIM EAT. Of course, he watched right back. It was like staring into a mirror. Well, not quite. But he would take a bite, she would take a bite. He'd sip his wine, she'd do the same. She echoed every gesture, paused with every pause. She was Ginger to his Fred; dancers with no music.

When he didn't react, she decided to crank it up a notch. Carefully, she put her fork down on the side of her plate, then made the *mmm* sound of appreciation, only real low and deep and sexy. Then, feeling quite foolish, but daring, too, she licked her upper lip, taking her own sweet time.

Nothing changed. His expression was exactly the same as— Hold on. Oh, my. He'd put his fork in his mouth, only he'd forgotten to pick up any food on it. And yet, he didn't seem to notice as he proceeded to chew and swallow.

Excellent.

She picked up her wineglass and took a tiny, quick lick of the rim before she sipped the chardonnay. As she'd anticipated, Chase's gaze was fixed on her mouth, on her tongue. Such a bad boy.

Next, she reached across the table to get the pepper mill, even though she had no desire for pepper. But she knew that when she stretched, her dress molded against her breasts. She didn't even have to look this time to sense where his gaze had wandered. Heck, this was like shooting fish in a barrel.

He cleared his throat and shifted his gaze. She'd see about that.

"These candles are really beautiful, aren't they."

His grunt sounded sort of like "Yes."

"I think the flickering light is so soothing. You know what one of my favorite things is?"

"I wouldn't even hazard a guess."

She smiled, although she didn't give him any teeth. "I love slipping into a nice, hot, wet...bubble bath."

No comment, except for the bobbing Adam's apple.

She sighed as she ran two fingers lazily up her arm. "I light my private candles and fill the tub with rose-scented bubble bath, then I sink down until my whole body is under the water, and my head rests on my bath pillow."

She took another sip of wine, giving him time to fine-tune his mental picture. "I close my eyes and let the water and the roses soothe away all my worries. All that's left to do is wash. I don't like to use a cloth or anything. I just get my hands all soapy. Of course, I start with my toes—the summer can be so harsh on bare feet. And then I work my way up to my ankles." She paused, milking the moment. "Then I move my hands to my legs and knees."

He swallowed again, his eyes slightly glassy.

"I lean back to wash my thighs, of course. Because I need to be comfortable and completely relaxed when I..."

Chase couldn't help it. He leaned forward, waiting for her to finish the sentence. And waiting. Dammit. What was she doing to him?

She took another sip of wine, then put the glass

down. He let out his breath, sure she'd go on, begging her to go on.

She twirled some pasta on her fork and brought it to her mouth. Opening her lips, the food slipped inside, and then her lips closed on the fork—and he had to look away before he started crying.

This wasn't amusing. She was doing it on purpose. All of it. He'd thought she was innocent. A babe in the woods. What a laugh. She was more like the big, bad wolf.

He took a deep breath and loosened the stranglehold he had on his glass before it shattered. He also wanted to loosen his pants before they burst at the seams, but that was a no-go because he was afraid to touch himself anywhere in the vicinity of his fly. A stiff breeze would probably push him over the edge, and on the list of tricks to impress your date, coming at the dinner table was below everything with the possible exception of choking and turning blue in the face.

There was only one other time in his life when he'd been in this much trouble. He'd been fifteen and, like most guys his age, he'd been a virgin. A hopeful virgin. He'd spent the summer at his friend Jeff's place, and Jeff had a cousin. Her name was Eve. She liked to tease him and, at seventeen, she was already a master.

One day she left the bathroom door open, just a tad. Just enough for him to peek inside. He hit the mother lode—Eve, who was built like a brick house, was taking off her bathing suit.

Years later, he realized she actually had been putting on a show for him, and that the door wasn't left open accidentally. At the time, he thought he'd died and gone to heaven.

Eve was the most gorgeous creature on the planet.

Blond, tall, with legs that went on for about a mile, she was the picture of feminine perfection in his eyes, a veritable Miss July, sprung fully formed from the pages of *Playboy* magazine.

His fifteen-year-old hormones went into overdrive. But before he could move away, Eve yanked open the door. She had somehow put a towel around her good parts, and she was furious.

He begged her not to tell. He didn't want to be banished to his parents' incredibly boring apartment back in Manhattan. He wanted to be with Jeff, and the pool and the goddess who had him by the T-shirt.

He'd begged, and she'd finally agreed to keep his secret, but only if he'd submit to being her slave for the rest of his stay.

The torture had been exquisite.

She'd made him rub lotion on her body, fetch drinks, give her massages, make her bed. And he'd had the erection that wouldn't die. It went on for days. Eve had wanted him to take off his clothes for her, but at that he put his foot down. It was bad enough that he had to wear two pairs of jockey shorts under his bathing suit just so he wouldn't give Jeff's mother a stroke, but there was no way he was going to show Eve his predicament in all its glory.

Of course, if he'd been just a bit older, he would have understood that her request wasn't the cruel trick he'd imagined, but a wicked introduction to the wonders of sex. Damn. He could have had a really great summer. Instead, it was full of pain and anguish and sweet suffering. Like tonight.

He wondered where Eve was now. She was probably a dentist or an island despot.

But because there was a great deal of humor in the

universe, he'd found himself another Eve. He was older now. Wiser. He knew perfectly well that Jamie was intentionally torturing him. That every move she made was meant to torment him. He was wise to the woman, no doubt about that. Unfortunately, his penis caught none of the nuances and, frankly, misunderstood the entire scenario.

"Chase?"

"Yeah?"

"Where have you been? I've been talking to you and you haven't heard a word I've said."

He smiled, although it was definitely not one of his best efforts.

"And you've hardly eaten a thing."

"I'm not very hungry."

"Did you have dinner before you came over?"

He shook his head.

"Then, you must be hungry. Go on. Just a few more bites, and we'll call it even."

He obeyed. Just like with Eve. He ate one bite, then two, not tasting anything, not seeing anything but Jamie's gaze, Jamie's soft cheeks, Jamie's lips.

He swallowed as she leaned toward him. What was going on? She kept leaning forward until they were only a breath apart. He closed his eyes, ready for her lips on his. Instead, she took her index finger and touched the corner of his mouth. Then she brought that finger to her lips and she sucked the tip. The symbolism wasn't lost on him. She closed her eyes and moaned. He moved, and she sat back in her seat as if she hadn't just come on to him in the most blatant, vivid, obvious maneuver since Marilyn Monroe sang "Happy Birthday."

"What was that?"

"You had some sauce on your mouth."

"In this country, it's traditional to use a napkin for that sort of thing."

"But what fun would that be?"

He sighed, wondering how things had gone so wrong so fast. She had him twisted around her little finger, when just an hour ago he'd had *her* on the edge.

Time for him to do something about it. Now. And the quickest way he knew to get her off balance was to kiss her senseless.

He stood up, went to her side, took hold of her arms and pulled her up. She stared at him in surprise. Good. Then he leaned down to capture her mouth.

Only, she wasn't there.

She'd slipped out, ducking beneath his arm so fast that he had no time to catch her. A moment later, she smiled victoriously, stretched, making sure she pushed out her chest, and yawned.

"How did it get so late? I can't believe how tired I am. It must be the pasta. All those carbs."

"What?"

"Thank you so much for the wonderful dinner." She took hold of his arm by both hands and headed toward the door. "Next time, I'll cook, but I'm not nearly as good as you are. I have a wonderful recipe for Asian chicken, though. Do you like chicken?"

"Uh—"

"Good. Then, that's settled. We'll have dinner."

"Hey—"

When they reached the door, Jamie stood on tiptoes and kissed him briefly on the lips. Then the door was open, her hand was on his shoulder, and he was outside.

"Good night," she said, just barely hiding her

amusement. She shut the door, and he listened to her lock all five of her dead bolts.

What in hell had she done to him? He checked his watch. Just after one in the morning. He'd planned to have her in bed by now, and look at him, standing like some schmuck on her doorstep, with nothing to show for the evening but an erection.

He thought of Dale Parker, his roommate at Yale. Thank God Dale couldn't see this mess. Dale used to brag that Chase could charm the panties off every female within five thousand feet without breaking a sweat. Tonight, he couldn't charm a scent from a rose.

It was crazy. The last time he'd been this bewildered by a woman, he'd been in puberty. It was Eve all over again. And while he was supposed to be the serpent, he'd ended up being the goddamn apple.

He thought of knocking, but decided against it. He'd go home, although it would be a few minutes until he could climb on his bike.

No wonder he'd been bamboozled. All the blood that should have been in his brain had migrated south.

JAMIE LEANED against the door, her heart slamming against her chest, her breath shaky and unreliable, her thoughts running a hundred miles an hour. She'd done it! She'd actually used some of her techniques and they'd worked.

Of course, what she hadn't anticipated was the backlash. There was a price to be paid for acting wickedly, and she was paying it now. If she looked up *horny* in the dictionary, she'd see her own picture.

Damn, but she'd been cool. She had to hand it to herself, she'd been one savvy babe. He'd panted over her, lusted for her, needed her—and all because she'd taken her own advice.

This was great. Better than great. She should have done this ages ago. She had so much more to tell her listeners now. Wait till they heard.

Chase Newman seducing her? Not likely. She was *the man!* Wait, that wasn't right. She was *the woman!* Yes, but what she meant was... She knew what she was. Smart. That's what. Smart and in control.

Be that as it may, she still had to deal with the, uh, repercussions. She couldn't possibly just go to sleep. First, she wasn't the least bit tired, and second... The way he'd looked at her. She closed her eyes and remembered. His dark, brooding eyes, his chiseled jaw, his perfect lips. He was a man built for sex, created for making love. If the situation were different, she'd be in his bed so fast she'd make the land speed record.

But it wasn't different. No matter how much her body wanted him, how much her mind kept imagining all the things they could do, she had to keep her distance. Stay one step ahead of him. Too much was at stake.

She pushed herself away from the door. The dishes needed washing. She should do it now, get it over with. She wasn't the kind to leave the place messy. Never had been.

No. Not tonight. Tonight she would say the hell with the dishes. The hell with everything except her fantasies. She might not be able to have sex with Chase, but it didn't mean she couldn't think about him.

Abandoning the kitchen and the remains of dinner, she headed for the bathroom. As she undressed, she closed her eyes, and he came to her in all his gorgeousness. When he smiled, he looked wicked and boyish at the same time. And his cheekbones! He reminded her of Johnny Depp, who was one of the most stunning creatures on the planet. But Johnny didn't have Chase's strong jaw. Or his sexy laugh. Granted, she hadn't kissed Mr. Depp, but she didn't think there was any way he could kiss her more sensually.

Her mind's eye moved down to Chase's chest. Perfectly broad, amazingly muscular, with exactly the right amount of hair. He was her dream date, her fantasy man, her dark stranger.

And he was absolutely, positively not going to be hers.

She brushed her teeth and washed her face in a fury, angry at what the fates had allowed. By the time she got to her bedroom and slipped on her T-shirt, however, her sense of outrage had diminished, replaced by the prospect of climbing between the sheets.

She'd always had a rich fantasy life, and although she might be inexperienced when it came to men, she wasn't a complete sexual novice. She'd learned early that it was perfectly fine to take matters into her own hands, and that, in fact, it was healthy physically and emotionally. More and more studies were touting the virtues of solo sex...

But her focus was far, far away from scientific theories. In fact, what she was feeling was as basic and undignified as it gets. She was going to sleep with Chase, all by herself.

She opened her nightstand drawer. In it were candles (perfect), aromatherapy oils (yummy), a book by Anaïs Nin, which she wouldn't need tonight (thank you, Mr. Newman), and her old standby Bob, her battery-operated boyfriend.

She lit two candles, put lilac scent in the glass diffuser designed to warm the oil, and lit the bottom of that. Then she slipped between her crisp, white sheets and turned the light off.

Sighing into her pillow, she watched the flickering shadows on her walls, just letting herself relax. As her breathing became more rhythmic and even, her eyes fluttered closed and her imagination kicked into gear.

Chase. With his hands on her shoulders. His warm breath on her neck. Her hand went to her panties and slipped inside. No Bob for her tonight—too impersonal. She wanted sensuality, erotica. She wanted to let go and allow her fantasies to carry her away.

She pictured him so clearly, right down to the slightly crooked tooth and the hint of five-o'clock shadow. His hands moved from her shoulders to her breasts, and she imagined with startling clarity his powerful fingers teasing her nipples, making them erect and painfully sensitive.

It was like watching a movie—but there was no plot, no script, just moving pictures and projected sensations. She let her own fingers work their magic as Chase pulled her dress up and off her, letting it drop where they stood. She was naked—no bra, no panties, just naked—and then so was he, and he took her breath away with his flawless physique. Her gaze moved down his chest, in no rush at all. She pictured his nipples, the chest hair that tapered to a *V*, his rippled abs and his innie belly button. Slim hips and strong, flat tummy.

Her breaths grew faster and more shallow as the sensations in her body shifted from pleasant to intense. It would be over too soon, but she couldn't slow down. The wave had started and there was no turning back.

She let her gaze move down, but before she could

see any more, he pulled her into his arms, into a kiss that made her moan. His lips, his tongue, his breath, his taste...it was so real, so perfect, and—

Tensing, she held her breath, letting the wave crest as she shuddered in a glorious climax. A moment later, after she'd gotten most of her equilibrium back, her eyes opened. Staring at the ceiling, at the shadows from the candles, she came to a terrible realization.

He'd ruined this for her. She'd always counted on being able to take care of herself, to exercise her fantasies, to give her sexual side its due. And once she had taken care of business, she could relax and get on with life. Only...tonight she'd climaxed but she didn't feel fulfilled.

Her imagination wasn't enough. She wanted the real thing. She wanted Chase.

She sat up and blew out the candles. As the darkness swallowed her, she laid back down and buried her face in her pillow.

He was ruining everything—her career, her future, and now this, the one thing she'd never questioned or worried about.

It wasn't fair. In fact, it was downright cruel.

CHASE STOOD at his window, watching the late-night traffic on Fifth Avenue. He should go to bed, get some sleep. He wasn't tired.

Jamie hadn't left him alone. Not even for five minutes. He'd finally been able to climb on his bike and drive back to the hotel, but once he'd parked, he didn't go up. Instead, he walked, block after long block, not seeing the window displays, barely noticing the people he passed, the cars, the sound of the horns.

She'd thrown him a sucker punch tonight.

Jamie had been frightened of him. He hadn't made that up. He distinctly remembered her darting glances, the way she shrank into the walls as he walked by. And when he'd pulled her into that alley, his intent was anything but noble. He liked seeing the shock in her eyes and, more than that, the pounding of her heart as he stood so close. She was frightened, as much of herself as of him. The game had been to awaken her, but now it seemed she'd been awake for years.

He wasn't usually wrong about women. Oh, he might miss the finer details but, on the whole, he knew what he was talking about. He'd given the matter of women almost as high a priority as he gave racing.

Was it the surprise that made him want her this much? She'd certainly pushed the right sexual buttons. He found himself becoming aroused at the very thought of her. The way those big, dark eyes had looked at him so hungrily. Her long, delicate neck. The way her breasts seemed to swell as her dress molded against her chest.

Dammit, he was doing it again. It was ridiculous. He'd left spontaneous erections back in high school, or so he'd thought.

He crossed his room and sat down on the edge of the bed. The phone message he'd scrawled was still on the nightstand. His manager wanted him to do an exhibition race in Paris next week. The offer couldn't have come at a better time. He'd leave New York on Sunday, and forget all about the radio joke and about Dr. Jamie. He loved Paris, and he hadn't seen Anna in almost eight months. Beautiful, blond Anna, whose estranged husband didn't understand her. Who was very good in bed.

He'd be wise to stick with the Annas of the world. Keep clear of the Jamies.

Not that he was totally giving up. He had till Sunday. Five days to find out if Dr. Jamie's bite was as bad as her bark.

He kicked off his boots, then finished undressing. In his boxers, he went to the bathroom, did his thing, and in short order he was in bed, the Do Not Disturb sign anchored on the door.

As his head hit the pillow, an image of Jamie came to him without his permission. In his mind, she looked at him through half-closed eyes, her lips moist and parted, and she was completely naked.

He hardly knew where to start.

8

"THIS IS DR. JAMIE, and we're talking about sex. Go ahead, Phil."

"I know you've been asked this before, but I don't know what I'm doing wrong. My wife isn't having orgasms—at least, not with me."

"How much time are you spending on foreplay, Phil?"

"I don't know. Five minutes?"

"And what does your foreplay consist of?"

He cleared his throat. "She usually goes down on me, and then I go down on her..."

"And this all takes place in five minutes?"

"Sometimes longer."

"I'm not sure this is going to solve your wife's orgasm deficiency, but I bet it helps. I want you to take notes on this, Phil, and study this. There will be a test."

"On what?"

"On the art of cunnilingus."

"Great."

"First, get comfy. Comfortable enough to hang out a while. Second, use your hands. Tease with your fingertips. Wet your fingers, then touch everything. Remember, lightly here. You're only revving the engines, not going in for a landing."

Phil laughed, but she could tell this was no joke to him.

"When she moves her hips, you can start with your tongue. Flick the tip of your tongue, or use the flat part like you're licking an ice cream cone. Try everything, and pay attention to her body language. After several minutes of casual exploration, focus in on the clitoris. And be careful about direct stimulation—she might be too sensitive. Again, pay attention to how she moves and what she says."

"Yeah. Okay."

"This would be a good time to use your fingers inside her. Find her G-spot, and if she likes that, keep it up as your tongue focuses on her. Increase your speed and pressure slowly. By this time, she's probably going to be thrashing about, so you'll have to keep up with her. Don't back off. Keep up the pressure as she gets close to her orgasm. Then, as soon as she comes, you move, quick like a bunny, and insert your penis. She's going to be swollen, and she'll love the feel of you inside her. Go for broke. She doesn't have to have another orgasm. She's fine. It's okay to concentrate on your own."

"Whoa. That's a lot of information."

"You sound like a bright guy. I bet you pick it up in two shakes."

"Great, I'll let you know what happens."

"Please do. And Phil? Go for it. Don't be shy. You'll enjoy yourself, too."

Marcy signaled that she had another caller on the line. When Jamie looked at her monitor, she felt a thump in her chest. Chase. He was on the phone. Why? *Why?* What did he want? She wasn't ready. Oh, damn, no. Not yet— "This is Dr. Jamie, and we're talking about—" she swallowed, forcing herself to calm down "—sex."

She pressed the button for line five. "Hello, Chase."

"Hello." His voice was so sexy, she knew they'd just climbed five points in the ratings.

"What's on your mind?"

"You."

She blushed, then willed the heat away. "And why is that?"

"At the moment because I'm staring at your face on the side of a bus. Actually, I'm staring at both our faces."

"Pardon?"

"Step outside on your next break," he said. "You'll see what I mean."

"So, uh, you saw this bus and it made you think of me?"

His laugh did something fluttery to her tummy. "That's not the only reason."

"What else?"

"Last night."

"Oh?" Her pulse was now at a steady clip of about a million beats per second. A part of her wanted to toy with him, to get sexy and intimate and just go with the flow. The other part of her was appalled at the knowledge that they were having this conversation with thousands of strangers listening.

"Did you tell them?"

"Tell them what?"

"About what you did?"

"No. I don't remember doing anything noteworthy."

"That's disappointing. I thought my linguini was quite noteworthy."

Her shoulders drooped. "I apologize. It was outstanding. Perfect."

"Then, why did you send me home?"

"It was late. I was tired."

"No, you weren't."

"You know better than I do when I'm sleepy?"

"I know quite a few things."

"Like?"

"I know how your nipples tighten when you're being kissed. I know the scent of you when you're aroused. I know that you didn't go right to sleep after I left, although I'll bet you went to bed."

The only reason Jamie didn't fall off her chair was that her headphones were attached to the console. "Ex—" She cleared her throat. "Excuse me?"

"Why don't you tell them what you did when you got in bed, Jamie."

"I went to sleep."

"Before that."

"That's personal."

"So you don't talk about that kind of thing on your show, eh?"

"Of course we do. It's perfectly natural. Nothing to be ashamed of."

He chuckled in that low, sexy way of his. "Then, you did satisfy yourself."

Dammit. He'd tricked her. "I didn't say that."

"Yes, you did, honey. You said that to me and about a hundred thousand of your closest friends."

Jamie fought her panic. Looking at Marcy didn't help. Her producer was on two phones at once, the phone bank was lit up like a Christmas tree, and Cujo was laughing his head off.

"So why don't you tell me what you thought about when you were in bed?"

"There's nothing to tell."

"You're lying, Jamie. And you don't do it very well."

"I think it's time for a commercial."

"The commercial can wait." His voice lowered. "Talk to me, baby."

She moaned as she buried her head in her hands. This was impossible, horrible. She was humiliating herself on the air again. The worst part of it was, she didn't know how to extricate herself from the situation with any kind of grace or wit. She felt thick and foolish, and if he called her baby one more time she was simply going to crawl under the console and never come out.

"Jamie?"

"What?"

"Look up."

She lifted her head. Chase, holding a cell phone to his ear, stood right next to Marcy in the production booth.

"Surprise."

"What are you doing here?"

"I thought your audience might like to know what *I* thought about last night when I went to bed."

"No."

"No?"

"Commercial. We must need a commercial now, right? Cujo? Marcy?"

Chase walked over to Cujo's board for a moment. The two men huddled, Cujo nodded, then Chase disappeared for a moment. Fred showed up in the production booth, and then her door swung slowly open. Chase's smile was victorious. He'd gotten her back for last night, all right. And then some.

She had to focus, shift the power. Last night had been so great, so intoxicating. She could do it again.

She had to. This was her playground, for heaven's sake. She was never uncomfortable talking about sex. "Come pull up a chair. Put on some headphones. I know my audience would love to hear about your night."

He slid into the chair next to hers, his air cocky, his scent intoxicating. "Where do you want me to start?"

"Why don't you set the scene for us. How do you sleep? Pajamas? Boxers?"

He shook his head. "In the raw."

"That makes things convenient. Do you use any kind of oil? Vaseline, maybe?"

He blinked, swallowed. Jamie had to force herself not to grin. The fly had voluntarily walked into her parlor, and now she had him in her web. No way he could embarrass her on the air.

"Chase?"

"No. No oils. No tricks, no equipment."

"Just your hand?"

"Uh, yeah."

"We've just spent some time giving some oral tips to our male listeners, and now it's time to switch gears. A lot of our female listeners want to understand how to give a really great hand job. It's always better to get that information directly from the horse's mouth, so to speak."

Chase coughed. He turned slightly away, but she'd already seen his blush. This was so great. She couldn't have asked for a more perfect situation.

His shoulders shifted back and he turned toward her. "I lick my palm," he said, slowly and distinctly, "then take hold of my penis at the base. Firmly. Then I move my hand up and down the shaft. I take my time, close my eyes and let my imagination go. Last night, you were the star of my private video. You were naked, and those nipples of yours were like thick pencil erasers, hard and sensitive and very, very pink.''

So he'd decided to fight fire with fire, eh? "And I'm sure you wouldn't mind sharing the dimensions of your penis? So that our listeners can get a visual."

He narrowed his eyes and shook his head, a warning. "A little over eight inches."

"Circumcised?"

"Yes."

"How thick? An inch? Two inches?"

"Closer to three."

"Oh, my. You must be very proud."

"I didn't build it. It came from the manufacturer this way."

She laughed, and then she looked at the window. Cujo was waving both hands at her, signaling for a break. Marcy, Fred and the intern were both on phones, and everyone who was still at the station at this late hour had come in to watch. Ted, of course—but also some of the computer techs, the program manager, his secretary and, if she wasn't mistaken, three of the cleaning staff.

"It seems we're late for a commercial, but I don't want to break right now. Cujo? Can we make this happen?"

Cujo turned to Fred. There was a very brief, very heated discussion, then Cujo pressed his mike button. He said to her and her audience, "It's your show, Jamie. Go for it."

"Wonderful." She turned to Chase. "You were saying?"

"I was saying that the act of masturbating is pretty much the same for all men. What varies is the fantasy.

And I've got a rich imagination. Last night, for example, in my mind, you were standing in front of me without a stitch on. And while you may be small, you still have curves in all the right places.'' He grinned. "I liked your haircut."

She touched the back of her head.

"Not that one." He winked at her. "That Brazilian look. Just that small strip of hair..."

He scored with that one. She hadn't seen it coming and she hadn't prepared her defense. What shocked her, what made it hard to come up with any words at all, was that he was right. She had gotten a Brazilian wax. It had hurt like hell, too.

"Were you peeking when you should have been cooking?" she finally managed to say.

The cocky smile was back. "No. But I knew, nonetheless. Just like I know that when you make love to yourself, you take your time. You like the feel of your own flesh. You don't like to admit it, Jamie, but your sensuality can't be hidden. Not by long, baggy dresses, or your degree. You need sex, baby." He leaned closer to her. "You need it or you'll wither and die."

The flutter in her chest stole her voice for a moment. Why did he have such an effect on her? They were just words. "No one, to my knowledge, has ever died from lack of sex."

"Maybe not physically, but emotionally, spiritually."

"So it's a spiritual experience for you?"

"Oh, yeah. If it's with the right woman."

"We're getting sidetracked here. This is Dr. Jamie, and Chase Newman is here in the studio talking to us about how he masturbates."

Chase's right eye twitched. He turned to look past

her, but she kept her eyes on him, forcing him to meet her gaze. He couldn't possibly be as cool as he'd like her to think.

"In Los Angeles, a colleague of mine, Dr. Susie, does her show from her bedroom. She invites guests to come on down, and everyone participates. Her guests get naked, and sometimes they get together right there, on the air."

"Are you suggesting we do that?"

"I was thinking that if you'd like, it would be fine if you wanted to get more comfortable. Maybe take those jeans off. Use all your senses as you explain the process. I'm sure my listeners would love it."

"I'll pass."

"They won't be able to see you, Chase. It is *radio*."

"How about the crew in there?" He nodded to the production booth.

"We can send everyone away except for Cujo and Marcy. Surely that wouldn't bother you."

"Hey, I'm game if you are."

"Oh, no. The host doesn't get naked."

"Why not? Is there something wrong with you? Or are you just embarrassed?"

"I'm perfectly comfortable with my body, thank you. But this show is about you tonight. You and you alone."

"Uh-uh. No go. But nice try."

She thought about taking one more dig, but perhaps she'd done enough. "Hmm. Okay. Sorry, ladies. Maybe next time."

He moved closer. "The next time I take off my pants, it's going to be for you, Doc. All for you."

"Isn't that nice."

He laughed. "Can I go on with my fantasy? Or are you just going to keep interrupting?"

"It's all yours."

"No. But it will be. And when you do give yourself to me, I'm going to teach you a thing or two. I know you have your degree and you've gotten straight *As* but, honey, there are some things you can't learn from books."

"Such as?"

"Such as what it feels like to come so hard your ears ring. You know what I'd do to you? I'd put you between my lips and suck you like an ice-cream soda."

Jamie opened her mouth but nothing came out.

"I'd tie you up so you couldn't move a muscle, and I'd put a blindfold on you, and then I'd play like a kid with a new toy. Nothing you could do but moan and come. And, honey, you would *come.*"

His eyes let her know this wasn't hypothetical, and it wasn't for the audience. He meant to do those things to her, and her body seemed to be enthusiastic about the idea. She wondered if Howard Stern or Dr. Susie had ever made love to a guest on the air. Maybe she could be the first.

"Jamie?"

From far away, she heard Marcy's voice. Turning slowly toward the window, Jamie saw Marcy point to her computer. It was a caller. A thirty-three-year-old from Soho. Somehow, Jamie managed to punch the right button. "Hi, Alicia. You have something to say?"

"I just wanted Chase to know that if you don't want him, I do."

"Thanks, sweetheart," Chase said, really pouring on the charm, "but Jamie does want me. She wants me more than she dares admit. And soon, very soon, she's going to ask me to make love to her.''

''I can't believe she hasn't already,'' Alicia said. ''I mean, come on. Who cares about a bet when she could be rolling in the sheets with you?''

''Why don't you ask her?''

''Okay. Dr. Jamie? Care to comment?''

Jamie stared at her console for a moment as she gathered her wits. She cleared her throat. Then, in what she believed was a very natural tone of voice, she said, ''Alicia, I'm glad you asked, because this wager isn't about who gets whom into bed first. It's about women and men, and the right to choose. To own up to our role in the mating dance, and to be cognizant that no one can trick us into doing anything we don't want to do.''

''Dr. Jamie?''

''Yes, Alicia?''

''That's such a crock. So what if he seduces you? It's not a crime unless you say no. I don't get the problem.''

''And that's why I can't afford to lose this bet. You see, Alicia, the struggle between men and women has been going on for hundreds of years. Since the time when we were nothing but property. We may not be owned by men in the strict sense any longer, but we're still under their thumbs. I talk to young women, women who should be having the time of their lives dating and playing the field, and you know what I hear over and over again?''

''What?''

''The young women are being seduced, but not by a man. By an idea. By the illusion that sex is love. It's not, and there isn't a man alive who doesn't know it.

That fantasy is in the feminine domain, and I can't tell you how many women have gone down in flames over it. Shall we talk about teenage pregnancy? Where do you think that starts? With the idea that we're helpless. That if he's trying to get me into bed, he must love me. And if I say yes, I'm saying I love him right back. Only, in the morning, there is no bond, no tie, no love. Just a guy and a girl with completely different agendas.''

"So, okay," her caller said, "I get that it can be that way, but isn't it possible that it can be magic, too?"

"Magic?"

"Yeah. Like in the fairy tales. Where it doesn't matter if she was seduced or not because they're meant to be together. They belong together."

Jamie didn't answer right away. "I suppose it could happen like that. It wouldn't be likely, but I'd be lying if I said I didn't think there might be a chance for magic."

"Great. So, um, how do you know?"

Jamie looked at Chase. "To tell you the truth, Alicia. I don't have a clue."

9

CHASE SAW the confusion on Jamie's face. It lasted a brief second, but it gave him his answer. Dr. Jamie was full of it. He'd suspected before; now he was sure. She talked a good game, but there was a fundamental flaw in her logic. Women weren't like men. They had not only different plumbing, but different wiring. And women, whether they liked it or not, were wired for committed relationships.

It made sense biologically. They needed to count on someone for food and lodging while they tended babies. Survival of the species.

While he did agree that some women could have sex for the hell of it, for the fun, with no strings and no expectations, such women were few and far between, and Jamie was not one of them.

It was a shame, because he'd thought a lot about how this little game was going to end. When he'd said yes, he'd wanted to show the good doctor a thing or two about sex and seduction and everything in between. But now that he was doing just that, the victory was bittersweet.

In the past two days, despite his best intentions, he'd come to like Jamie. Last night had clinched that. She'd be dangerous if she realized her own power. With that quick mind and that sinful body, she could make any man jump through hoops. That's what women in general didn't understand—Jamie, in particular.

Men wanted sex for the release, sure, but being inside a woman was the safest place on earth. No amount of money, power or glory could give a man that sense of security. Hell, men made money and became powerful just so they could get the women.

"Chase?"

He realized Jamie had been trying to get his attention. He'd been so lost in thought that he'd missed the commercials and her station ID. They were on the air. "Yeah?"

"Carly asked an interesting question."

"I'm sorry, I didn't hear it. I was distracted."

"That's all right. Carly, would you like to ask your question again?"

"Sure," came the sultry, low voice from the speaker. "I think women can have sex without love, but they don't want to. I think love is the whole purpose. I wondered what you thought about that?"

"Hmm." He had to be careful about this. The game was still afoot, and even though the outcome was more uncertain than ever, he didn't want to say anything that would mess things up. "I think love means different things to different people. If you're talking about security, then I agree."

"Love isn't security," the caller said, then chuckled softly. "Or, at least, it's a really small part of it."

"Fair enough." Chase leaned forward, closer to the mike. "So what is love?"

"I have no idea," Carly answered. "I've never been in love. Not really. I've been in like, and sometimes in lust, but never in love."

"How do you know?"

There was a pause. Jamie looked at him questioningly. "I think that's a very important question," she said.

"Here's what I think," Carly said. "I think that love is a spiritual, physical and emotional experience, like a three-legged stool. You take one of those aspects away, and the whole thing tips on its side. The secret is to find the balance."

Jamie closed her eyes for a few seconds. Then she smiled. "Carly, are you trying to take my job?"

"No. At least, not right now. I'm just trying to do this life thing well."

"From where I sit, you're doing one hell of a good job. I thank you for sharing with us."

"May I ask Chase one more thing?"

He nodded. "Shoot."

"What is it you know about women that makes you so good at seducing them?"

He opened his mouth to say something clever, but thought better of it. This woman was bright and thoughtful and she deserved an answer. So did Jamie.

"Every woman is unique. They don't get much credit for that. Every woman has a story that's hers alone, but I don't think many people listen to it. Women want to be heard. They want someone to pay attention to them, and I'm not just talking about sexually."

Jamie leaned in, but he put his hand up. He wasn't finished. "I also believe women want to be seduced. They want to pretend they don't have the responsibility. That the choice was taken from them." He looked at Jamie, not surprised to find her expression hardening.

"The thing is, women are responsible for so damn

much. They have to take care of the house, of the kids, of the cats, of the groceries, the dry cleaning, the car pools—the list goes on and on. This starts young—real young, from what I can see. Men are out there learning to compete, and women are taking up the slack. They always have. When it comes to love, and even just sex, I think women don't want to have to be the responsible party. For once, they want someone else to do it for them. To make it easy. To take the blame if things get messed up."

"And, believe it or not, I agree with you," said Jamie. "Women don't want the responsibility, so they give it away. Only, it's not that easy. They still get stuck with the consequences of their actions, whether they pretend to choose or not."

"Everybody gets stuck with the consequences, Jamie. That's life."

"So why should women bury their heads in the sand over this one issue?"

"I don't think you give your women friends enough credit. I think they all know what the real story is. They know. But sometimes even the toughest broad needs to be swept away."

"But—"

"You need to be swept away, darlin'. You need it badly."

She opened her mouth but didn't speak, and then Carly spoke up. "Chase?"

"Yes?"

"Fascinating answer. Thank you. Now, can you tell me why you don't have someone in your life? If you know women so well, why aren't you married? Or at least in love?"

"Okay, this is where I stop. I'll tell you all about

how I spank the monkey, but I won't tell you about why I'm not married. It's too personal.''

Carly laughed. "Fair enough. Thanks, Dr. Jamie and Chase. This was great."

"Thank you, Carly," Jamie said, then nodded at Cujo as she launched into her station ID segment.

While she was still talking, Chase excused himself and went down the hall to the employee lounge. There, he stared at the vending machines until his vision blurred. He wasn't thinking about cocoa or candy bars. His thoughts were with Jamie, and the simple question Carly had asked.

Like her, he'd never been in love, just lust. Or like. But mostly lust. He wasn't allowed the luxury of love, not because he couldn't feel it but because he knew what would happen if he did fall. He'd want what everyone wants—a life, a future, which he couldn't have.

It had never really bothered him. He'd accepted his fate years ago, when he'd discovered the facts about his great-grandfather's death. He could fight lots of things, but heredity wasn't one of them.

So why did he feel uneasy? Because the questioning on the air had come too close to the bone? A long time ago, he'd told a woman friend about his history, and his future, whatever there was going to be of it. She'd laughed and told him he was ridiculous. He'd never brought it up again. People didn't understand. They didn't know about the Newman men.

It wasn't a great tragedy. At least he knew his life wasn't going to go on forever, and he lived accordingly. So what if he'd never know what it was like to love a woman, to have her love him back. It didn't make any difference. Not really.

But as he got out his wallet, retrieved a dollar bill and fed it to the soda machine, a dark, solid fist of regret settled in his gut.

JAMIE ALMOST TOLD Chase to leave after the show. She was tired in a way that had little to do with sleep. The broadcast had been thoughtful—thanks to Carly and a few others—which should have pleased her. Instead, it just made her more insecure.

Just days ago, she'd been happy. Her show was doing well—her parents thought she was wasting her time and talent, but she believed she was helping people— and she'd made peace with her loneliness.

Now, as she stood in the bathroom of WXNT staring at herself in the mirror, her show was a publicity farce, and the one secret that could destroy everything was threatening in a very real way. Her mother had called this afternoon to ask her if she wanted to talk. Her mother never wanted to talk unless it was to share observations about what Jamie was doing wrong. Of course, the publicity had mortified her parents. They had only been enthusiastic about her radio career after she'd convinced them that her services were of real value. She wasn't sure of that now. Was she helping people? Was it right to tell women they had to take responsibility for every aspect of their lives? What if Chase was right?

The door swung open and Marcy walked in. "I've been looking for you. Chase has a car downstairs."

"I know. I don't think I'm going to go with him."

"How come?" Marcy watched Jamie's reflection as she washed her hands.

"I'm tired. I want to spend some time alone. No one said I had to be with him every day."

"You're right, although you're going to have to explain yourself to your listeners. Are you prepared to do that?"

"They'll understand."

Marcy grabbed a few paper towels and dried her hands. "Are you sure? They're having fun with this, Jamie. They want you to play."

"They can't want me to play that badly. Surely they'll forgive me for one night."

"You're so young," Marcy said, patting her on the shoulder. "You still think well of the masses. That's sweet."

"Cut it out, Marcy. I'm serious."

Marcy's smile faded. "What's wrong?"

Jamie leaned against the counter and debated her next words. "I'm confused. It's no big deal."

"Confused about what? Chase?"

She nodded. "And how I feel about him."

"Go on."

What the hell. "I have no intention of letting myself be seduced. I don't believe in it, and that's no line—I truly don't."

"But?"

"But every time I see the man my entire body goes wiggy on me."

"Explain 'wiggy.'"

"This is so embarrassing."

"Talk."

Jamie hopped up on the counter. Her skirt, a pale blue, gauzy number she'd picked up at a flea market, fanned around her knees. Her sandal-clad feet swung back and forth, making her feel about five. "I get butterflies in my stomach. I forget to breathe. I keep touching my hair and blushing and stammering and doing

all the stupid adolescent things a girl does when she
has a crush on a boy."

"And this surprises you?"

"Yes."

"Why?"

"Marcy, it's me. The one who doesn't believe in
seduction, remember?"

"Oh, come on, Jamie. Did you honestly think you
wouldn't feel anything for Chase? Any red-blooded,
heterosexual woman would..." Marcy raised a brow.

"No. I'm not gay."

"Well, then, what did you expect? He's stunning.
He exudes masculinity. He's smart, he's clean, he's
rich. He's everything you could want in a man, and, if
you haven't noticed yet, he has really big feet."

"Jeez, Marcy."

"It's important."

"That's not what I tell my listeners."

"My point exactly."

"Now you're being obscure."

Marcy jumped up on the counter next to Jamie.
"Look, kiddo, I think you're right to help women, especially young women, learn to accept responsibility
for their actions. If they're not hearing that message
from their parents, they're pretty much SOL. School
isn't teaching them. TV isn't teaching them. So you're
doing a good and noble thing."

"But?"

"But he's Chase Newman, and you'd have to be jug-
head stupid not to want him to seduce the hell out of
you."

"Jug-head stupid?"

Marcy grinned. "Okay, so I'm exaggerating, but not
by much. The man is the hottest thing since French

toast. You've heard the stories about him. Not only is he hot, but he's one of the good guys. He may be playing this out, but, in the end, he'll do the right thing."

"How do you know?"

"You know what Fred told me?"

"What?"

"Chase found out that Fred's daughter had a major crush on one of the Backstreet Boys. A week later, it's her birthday, and who comes to the station?"

"A Backstreet Boy."

"Exactly. It took Fred weeks to finally figure out it was Chase who'd used his father's connections to pull it off. Now tell me, is this not a wonderful guy? Honey, he wants you. And the butterflies in your tummy are saying you want him. What's the problem?"

"Are you suggesting I let him win?"

"It doesn't have to be anyone's business but your own."

"Lie to my listeners? Are you crazy?"

Marcy made a sour face. "Maybe. All I know is, Carly was right. You're not leaving any room for magic."

"I can't have it both ways."

"Let me ask you something. If you win this bet out of sheer willpower, have you really won?"

"What?"

"Seems to me that he has seduced you. You want it. If it weren't for the wager, I think you'd go for it. So, haven't you lost already?"

Jamie climbed down. "No. You're missing the whole point. It's about our actions, not our thoughts. I can wish a hundred times a day to be a jewel thief, but they can't arrest me until I take the diamonds."

"You are, aren't you?"

"What?"

"Thinking about him a hundred times a day. Call me crazy, but I think there's more than just sex and seduction going on between you two."

Jamie wanted to deny the allegation. But she was afraid Marcy was right—not that she would let her friend know that.

Marcy shrugged. "Have it your way."

"I intend to."

"So are you going to go with him?"

"No." She went to the door. "Yes." She pushed it open, then stepped into the hallway. As the door swung shut, she whimpered. "Maybe."

Marcy's droll "You go, girl!" made Jamie whimper one more time as she headed toward her office to get her things so that she could meet Chase.

The thought made her body quiver and her head ache. She was completely screwed.

CHASE HELD THE DOOR to his suite so that Jamie could enter. He'd taken a quick glance, and when he saw the dinner set up, he relaxed. The GM of the hotel had taken care of his requests, as always. It's why he stayed here when he could have picked any hotel in the city. If he wanted a dinner for two from one of the finest chefs in New York at midnight, voilà, it appeared. And they said money couldn't buy happiness.

"Wow. Look at this place." Jamie had zeroed in on the view, naturally. The panorama never failed to thrill. The city looked like something out of a dream from this height. A lesson there—anything can look pretty if you're far enough away.

"Is that dinner? Or breakfast?"

"Dinner. For us." He tossed his keys on the dresser. "Want some champagne?"

"Champagne gives me a headache."

"Not this champagne."

"Why not?"

"Trust me."

"Fine. Pour away."

He lifted the bottle and checked the label. As requested, it was a 1990 Cristal. Worth every penny of its exorbitant price. He popped the cork, then poured into the flutes. The sound of the bubbles made him sigh. Damn, what a great sound.

He took Jamie her glass and watched her expression as she sipped the chilled liquid. He doubted she realized her forehead was furrowed, probably in anticipation of bitterness. Sure enough, the moment she swallowed, her eyes widened in surprise. "Oh my God."

He nodded. "Welcome to great champagne."

"Very nice." She drank again, a bigger sip.

"Don't chug it. Even if it does taste like heaven it can still make you drunk."

She smiled. "You love this, don't you."

"What?"

"Showing me how sophisticated you are. How worldly."

He nodded. "I suppose I do."

"May I make a conjecture?"

"Why not?"

"Okay." She turned to face him, putting her glass on the coffee table. "I don't fully understand why you wanted to play this game with me, but I'm beginning to get an idea."

"Oh?"

"I think if it's all a game, then it's safe. You don't

have to worry. There's an end in sight, and I think that's all that's important to you.''

Chase's stomach clenched. She was right, more dead-on correct than she'd ever know. The end was in sight. The end of it all. The end of hearing her laughter. Of watching her eyes widen in surprise. Of touching that smooth, silky skin behind her knees.

He was going to miss that, and so much more. He put down his own glass as he moved to her side. His hand went to her hair and then to her cheek. The softness killed him. The sweet scent of her. The way she sighed.

He pulled her into his arms, wanting to touch her everywhere. To feel everything. He wanted her naked, open, waiting for him. He wanted the safety of being inside her, the immortality of those moments before his climax. All of the important things in life were right here, in this woman and, God forgive him, he couldn't let her go.

He kissed her, and when she trembled he knew she understood what he was asking her to do. The taste of her and the slight hint of champagne went right to his head. He stopped thinking, stopped worrying about anything but this moment.

He lifted her, sweeping his arm under her legs, and he carried her past the dinner under the silver domes, past the bar, through the door and to the bed. He put her down on her knees, so he wouldn't have to stop kissing her. Her tongue darted in his mouth, and when he returned the favor she sucked on him, giving him a sample of what she could do to far more sensitive places on his body.

His hand ran down her back and cupped her buttocks as he climbed on the bed in front of her. Face-to-face, on their knees, he pulled her toward him so she pressed against his jeans. Her soft gasp let him know she'd felt his erection straining for release. Soon, soon.

But first, he moved his mouth to the hollow of her neck, then to the curve below her ear. He licked, nibbled, kissed—lost in sensation, in the softness of her skin.

The world narrowed to a very small space. To a king-size bed and a small woman with too many clothes on.

His hands went to her blouse, pale blue, and her buttons. He undid three, and then he looked down to see she wasn't wearing a bra. The sight of her hard little nipples made him moan in a mixture of pain and pleasure too intense for one man to stand.

Dipping his head, he kissed the top of her breast, then slowly, slowly moved down, his tongue drawing a moist line to her bud. He captured her between his lips, ran his tongue in a tight circle, then sucked deeply.

She mewed as her head fell back. Her hands held his upper arms, her fingers digging in as she fought for balance. He wanted to shake her equilibrium, to make her feel as out of control as he did.

He needed her. He *needed.*

Jamie bit her lip to stop another moan. What he was doing to her! His lips, his tongue—she'd never felt anything like it before. No one had ever... Not even this. Her body was so unschooled, so naive. And under his tender ministrations she was coming alive, blooming as a new flower.

She held on to him as he suckled her right breast, then her left. The sensation was beyond anything she could have predicted. Everything in her was connected. Her nipples and her fingertips and her tummy and, most of all, between her legs. The more he touched her, the more she wanted to be touched. The more she wanted to give herself completely.

He nipped her lightly on the underside of her breast, and then she felt his hand on her leg, his fingers trailing a skittery line up onto her thigh.

She should stop him. She should. And she would, in a minute. In…just a few minutes.

He tickled her inner thigh, and then he moved his mouth from her breast to her lips. His kiss, soul deep and brazen, ignited another fire inside her. She'd been dry kindling, waiting for a match. And he'd hit her with a blazing torch.

Tongues dueled, fingers grasped, and her heart beat so fast it felt as if she would die from pure pleasure. And then his fingers were on her inner thigh, and while his tongue thrust inside her, his fingers moved to one panty leg, and slipped underneath. She had to stop him. Only, only…

His fingers brushed her sex, just a light, feathery brush that changed everything. But she couldn't…

She pulled away from his kiss, opened her eyes, tried to focus, to pull herself together, but his finger slipped inside her and he rubbed back and forth before settling on the perfect spot. Her mouth refused to do anything but moan as he rubbed tiny circles, making her whole body tremble and sway.

"Chase—"

"Hush."

She shook her head. "No. I can't."

"You can. We can. I feel how much you want it, Jamie. Did you think I couldn't tell? You're wet and hot and swollen and ready, and I'm going to make you scream."

"No."

"Say yes, Jamie. Just that one word. Say yes, and I'll take you straight to heaven."

"I—"

Just as she was about to push herself away, his finger plunged inside her. Not far, though. Her virginity stopped him short.

She shoved him back so hard that she nearly toppled. Instead, she scrambled to her feet and tried to button her blouse with useless hands.

"Jamie?"

She turned around, her face blazing with humiliation.

"My God, Jamie, tell me what that was."

"I have to go."

He was beside her then, and his hands on her shoulders turned her to face him. "Are you a virgin?"

She couldn't say it. She couldn't. All she wanted to do was disappear. Why had she let it get this far? She was stupid! Stupid, and foolish, and now it was all over. Everything. Her life, her career. She'd be the laughingstock of New York.

"Jamie?"

She swallowed hard and nodded. If she could have come up with a lie, she would have, but her brain had stopped functioning.

His head tilted to the side as he gazed at her in utter confusion. "But you're Dr. Jamie, the Sexpert."

"No. I'm Dr. Jamie, the fraud."

10

CHASE FOLLOWED HER out of the bedroom, his mind still trying to fold around this startling bit of information. *A virgin.* The thing was, he'd just blurted it out, not really believing he was right. But the look on her face...

Jamie had never had sex.

She grabbed her purse and headed toward the door. He tried to stop her, but she was too quick for him and shut the door in his face. He didn't let that stop him. A second later, he was in the hallway running after her. She couldn't leave. Not yet. Not until he got to the bottom of this.

At the elevator, she pressed the down button a half-dozen times, and as he got closer he saw a tear glisten on her cheek. A pang of something—guilt? compassion?—hit him where it counted.

"Please leave me alone," she said, her voice choked with pregnant sobs.

"I can't. Come back with me. We can talk about this."

"No."

"Jamie, it doesn't—"

She faced him squarely so he could see the pain distort her face. "Go ahead. Say it. I'm a fraud. I am. It's true. So now you know. Now everyone will know. I don't give a damn. I'm tired of pretending. Go call

Whittaker. She'll be thrilled. She'll probably get a damn Pulitzer for her exposé.''

"I have no intention of calling her."

The elevator door opened, and Jamie slipped inside. "I don't care. Do whatever you like."

He blocked the door with his body. "Just come back."

"No."

"Please."

She squeezed her eyes shut for a moment. When she opened them, the anguish made his chest ache. "I can't talk to you now."

He nodded. Stepped back. "I'll call you," he said as the door closed.

A virgin. He still couldn't quite get it. The most famous sex therapist since Dr. Ruth had never had sex. No, wait. He couldn't be sure about that. She'd never had intercourse. She might have done everything else under the sun. She sure as hell talked like she had. But now he wasn't sure of anything.

As he headed back to his room, he dug his card key out of his pocket. Man, if Darlene got wind of this—

A thought hit him between the eyes. Darlene had suspected. Not necessarily this, but something. Of course she had. That's why she'd been so determined to see this prank through. Why she'd been so convincing when she'd asked him to seduce Jamie. What he didn't understand was what had made Darlene suspect there was a secret. Something had tipped her off, he felt sure of that. A man? A scorned lover? What was the woman trying to prove?

He should have thought of all this before he'd agreed to be Darlene's patsy. He'd never guessed that this might be the outcome, but he should have realized there were ulterior motives at work. He wasn't some rube. He knew people were selfish. Hell, hadn't he agreed to this out of selfishness himself? Sure. He wanted to sleep with Jamie. Who cared what *she* wanted? He had something to prove.

He walked into the suite. Dinner was still warm under the silver domes. Filet mignon with truffles, prepared by one of the best chefs in the country. No need to waste it all, right?

He sat down, removed the dome in front of him and stabbed a baby potato with his fork. Decidedly not hungry, he ate the side dish anyway, then the steak. Despite his lack of enthusiasm about the meal, he had to admit it was incredible. Jamie would have been impressed.

He reached over and grabbed the champagne from the ice bucket, brought the bottle to his lips and tipped his head back.

Not a smart move. He coughed for several minutes and then gasped for breath. Impetuous. That's what he was. Greedy. Selfish.

Everything was always about him, no one else. The excuse he used to justify his behavior had always felt solid: death at thirty-five was a powerful motivator. But it was an excuse—a way to rationalize his actions, no matter how reprehensible.

He'd put Jamie in a terrible position. She'd never be syndicated now, not after this got out. She probably wouldn't work in radio again.

All because he'd wanted to prove he was a stud. It wasn't about boredom, not completely at least. He'd wanted everyone to see he was *the man* in the bedroom. Dammit, his ego was that big.

He lost his appetite for everything but the champagne. He grabbed the bottle in one hand, the glass in the other, then leaned back.

What was he supposed to do now? He didn't have any desire to hurt Jamie, although he already had done so. He didn't want her career to go down the tubes because he was a jerk. Should he lie? Should he just tell Darlene that Jamie had won? That he hadn't been able to seduce the doctor?

He took a drink, and when he didn't choke, he finished the glass and poured himself another, all the while thinking about what it would be like on the circuit once he'd admitted defeat. Oh man, the drivers would have a field day. He'd be the butt of jokes for years to come.

Maybe there was a compromise. A way for both Jamie and him to win. He'd have to think this thing through carefully. And he would, as soon as he had another glass of champagne. Or two.

JAMIE HAD NO IDEA where she was. She'd been walking for hours, barely aware of the traffic or the late-night pedestrians or even of the balmy night air. Her tears had finally slowed to a trickle, and she supposed she should be grateful for that. There was nothing else to be grateful for.

She'd blown it—blown it to smithereens. Her career, her future, her reputation, her credibility—all gone because she'd let herself be seduced. The irony burned like a white-hot brand.

A red light stopped her, and while she waited, she forced herself to tell the truth. There was no such thing as seduction. She had walked into Chase's suite with her eyes wide open. He hadn't done anything she hadn't given him permission to do. She hadn't been hexed or hypnotized or enticed or led astray. Whatever happened—all of what happened—it was her own weakness, her own vulnerability, her own stupidity that had been to blame.

Was it worth it? Was having him touch her worth more than her career?

Her gait slowed as she turned a corner. She thought about the moment he'd put her on the bed. When he'd kissed her and teased her and… She hadn't been thinking about the wager or her job or anything else. Being with Chase had shifted her focus to a very old and basic part of the brain. The place where there were no consequences, where there was no rationale or logic. Just need and supplication, heat and moisture. Primal.

The time for her to have stopped him was way before the bedroom. That's where she should have been strong. Dammit, she never should have gone with him to the hotel. Some part of her had to have known what was going to happen.

A bus rumbled by, and even in the dark she could see the artwork on the side. It was a picture of Chase and a picture of her, superimposed so that they appeared to be gazing into each other's eyes. Her stomach lurched as the bus screeched to a halt about fifty feet in front of her.

Turning abruptly, she headed blindly down the street, the shame so acute that she thought she might throw up. What had she done? How could she possibly face anyone?

She should leave, that's all. Get on a plane heading anywhere, and start again wherever she landed. She could do that. Maybe she could be a secretary. One thing was for sure: she couldn't be a call girl. Not with no experience.

She spied a bench in front of a church, and when she got there, she sank down gratefully. The area registered—she was at St. Mark's Place. Miles from home, but so what? Home, comfort, security—they were all transitory. A moment's indiscretion and, *poof,* they could all be taken away. God, what would her parents say?

Not that they'd be unhappy she was a virgin. They were her parents, after all, but the public humiliation would hit them hard. They'd hated her being on the radio in the first place, and she had a feeling, although neither of them had ever said it, that they would have preferred her using a pseudonym. They didn't want to be associated with the show, or her. She could see it in her mother's eyes.

Now they'd really have something to be ashamed of. Wait until Whittaker's article came out. Oh man. It hurt to think about it.

She could have had sex on several occasions. Okay, that wasn't true; she could have done it twice. Once in high school, when the boy she tutored, a gangly basketball player with unfortunate skin, had groped her at his living room table. And once in college, when Mitch Madden had asked her to go to the midnight performance of *Rocky Horror Picture Show.*

Fool that she was, she'd turned them both down. She should at least have considered her options, especially with Mitch. He'd been really good-looking, and experienced. But, no, she had to run and hide in her books, too scared even to date.

She didn't deserve her show. She didn't deserve her degree. Maybe it was just poetic justice. She'd felt like a fraud all her adult life, and now the rest of the world would agree.

Sighing deeply, she wondered yet again how she'd let things get so out of control. She wasn't a fool, but she certainly had been foolish when it came to Chase. If only his touch hadn't made her shiver, if his voice didn't set off all sorts of wild fantasies. Every time she thought of him, her body reacted, and when she was with him, it got ten—no, a hundred—times worse.

At least now she understood what women meant when they claimed to be victims of seduction. To the unwary, the physical symptoms of attraction could feel overwhelming. But feeling flushed and having butter-flies in the tummy did not mean one had to swoon into a man's arms and let him have his way.

It was tempting, though, to abandon all responsibil-ity, to be swept away on an ocean of lust.

She wanted him. She wanted him in a way that was completely foreign to her. It had nothing to do with her intellect, with her rational mind. Her body felt in-complete, yearning to be whole. Her breasts ached, and that was the least of her problems. She squeezed her legs together, trying to ease the discomfort there, but it was useless. There was only one thing that could fix her.

She watched a stretch limo pass by, the darkened windows hiding its secrets. Maybe there were lovers inside, doing naughty things while the driver tried not to look.

Maybe now that Chase knew the truth, she could take that next step. Risk what she'd never been willing to risk before. Maybe it was her turn to live life rather than talk about it.

On the other hand, he probably wanted nothing to do with her. He'd seen her for the phony she was. He and Whittaker were probably having a real good laugh about now.

Jamie sniffed and rubbed her eyes with the palms of her hands. She'd best get used to being laughed at—and staying a virgin. Welcome to the end of the world as she'd known it. Welcome to utter failure.

SHE HADN'T ANSWERED her phone or called him back, even though he'd left a half-dozen messages. So Chase had no choice but to go to the radio station that evening.

His day had been one of unanswered questions, the first of which was why he'd felt compelled to finish the champagne. But after a shower, aspirin and a hot meal, the real quandary surfaced. He had no idea what to do, how to handle things. It wasn't like a race, where there were rules and flags and clear winners and losers. This situation was the kind he always tried to avoid. In truth, he never got close enough to anyone to find himself embroiled in their lives. He was the kind of guy you could completely depend on if everything was going well—which had made a lot of sense to him for a lot of years. Only, last night and today, some strange ideas had popped into his head.

What would his life have been like if he'd gone the other direction? Instead of keeping aloof, guarding himself against making connections, what if he'd put himself out? What if he'd let himself care? Let himself need?

After nodding at the receptionist, a woman he didn't recognize, he headed down the long hallway. With each step, he grew more convinced that he was losing his mind. He'd be gone in a few years—why bother getting involved with Jamie? What did he care what happened to her?

But as he rounded the door into the production booth, he was hit hard, right in the chest. He didn't want to hurt her. He didn't want to blow her secret.

Cujo grinned at him from behind the board. "Hey, lover boy. I heard about you on WGNX this afternoon. They had a whole discussion about the bet. And half the women calling up said they'd do ya. Man, some dudes have all the luck."

Chase smiled even though he didn't feel the least bit lucky. Confused, yes, but lucky?

He turned so he could see Jamie. She was nearly hidden by the big fuzzy microphone and the console, but he could see half of her face. Her pale skin, those huge brown eyes, that tousled hair. Something inside him tensed, and it wasn't just because she was beautiful. There were dark circles under her eyes. She wasn't herself. The pain and defeat of last night had changed her posture and aged her face.

He had a lot to be proud of. He'd hurt her, now held the potential of ruining her whole career—and for what? Because he was such a jackass. He had to prove he could seduce the indomitable Dr. Jamie. But he didn't feel victorious. He felt like crap.

"Hi, Chase."

He turned toward Marcy and managed a smile. "How are you?"

She glanced at Ted, who was standing by the row of tape boxes reading the labels. "I'm fine."

"How's Jamie doing?"

"Okay. Why?"

"No reason."

She gave him a questioning glance, but then Ted

walked past her and her attention shifted. Chase watched her stare at the DJ, and it was damn clear that she was attracted to the guy. Chase guessed Ted was at least five years younger than Marcy, but she didn't care. She looked at him like he could fix what ailed her, and give her a smile to boot.

Chase glanced at Jamie, but then Marcy headed toward Ted and Chase had to admit he was curious. She was going to say something, ask Ted a question. But it was none of his business.

Only, it was kind of hard to miss. They were real close, too close for him to get up now without disturbing them. He just wouldn't listen, that's all.

Marcy touched the back of her hair. She looked at the floor, at the ceiling, then at the floor again. She cleared her throat, and even though Chase refused to look, he was pretty sure she was blushing.

"Come on, girl," he whispered to himself. "Go for it." Oh, hell. He had to look, just a little.

As if his words had spurred her on, she smiled brightly. "Ted?"

Ted turned to her, his face the essence of cluelessness. The man had no idea he was being pursued. Did any man, ever?

"Yeah?" he replied.

"I was thinking about, um…I was, uh, wondering…"

Ted's brows came down as he tried to decipher the conversation.

"Lunch," she finally blurted. "I was thinking about lunch."

Ted's right brow arched. "Yes?"

"Maybe you'd like to, uh, have some."

"Lunch?"

She nodded.

"With you?"

Another nod, this one breathless, from what Chase could see.

"When, tomorrow?"

"Yes."

"Sure. That'd be great."

Marcy's shoulders relaxed as she let her breath out. "Great. Then I'll call you. We can go to Union Pacific, if that's okay."

He nodded, but his face showed none of Marcy's eager infatuation. In fact, Ted looked a little bored. Too bad. Marcy was a nice woman. Attractive, too. And she wanted him so much. She should have asked him for dinner, not lunch. Lunch was business. Lunch was an expense account. Dinner at least had the potential for dessert. For after-dinner drinks.

"I'll make a reservation," she said, but Ted was looking at the door, his attention slipping away with each passing second.

"Great. I'd like that. But, hey, let's talk about it later, okay? I've got to make a phone call."

"Sure," Marcy said with a grin that was as real as Anna Nicole Smith's boobs.

Ted didn't catch it. He just headed toward the door. He stopped, though, just after he stepped into the hallway. "Marcy?"

"Yes?"

"Why don't you make those reservations for dinner?"

Her smile changed completely. In fact, the woman fairly beamed. Ted grinned back, and Chase knew he'd had it all wrong. Ted, the old dog, had just been playing it cool. He knew the score.

Marcy floated across the room, unaware, he assumed, of her silly grin. His own lips curled, and he tried to convince himself that he was just reacting to their situation. That he didn't understand that feeling, that lightness.

Shit, he was in bigger trouble than he'd thought. What in hell was he supposed to do now? How about not taking himself so damn seriously? Come on, this wasn't the end of the world. The girl was a virgin—so what? In some cultures, that was considered a virtue.

A commercial for a local furniture store came on, and he remembered the first night he'd ever seen Jamie. He'd surprised her in the hallway, by the archives. She'd nearly jumped out of her skin. After the initial shock, as they'd stood side by side at the file cabinets, she'd looked him over, and then, as he watched, her cheeks had turned pink, her lush lips had opened and she'd leaned toward him. Not so much that she would have fallen, just enough to tell him she was drawn to him. And the surprise in her gaze turned to fear—and something more. He hadn't thought about it until now, but he remembered feeling as though she wanted to kiss him—that in the next second, she'd be in his arms.

It hadn't happened. A door had slammed somewhere, and she'd bolted like a fawn into the forest.

He leaned to his right so he could see more of her behind her equipment. And it occurred to him why he'd remembered that incident after all this time. Last night, on his bed, she had had that same look in her eyes. That half frightened, half hungry stare that made him instantly hard.

She might be a virgin, but she wasn't happy about

it. She needed to make love, and it had nothing to do with her radio show.

He was the man for the job. It was going to be fantastic.

11

JAMIE PUSHED the mute button and turned the show over to Cujo. She couldn't believe she'd made it through the first two hours. Her thoughts were scattered, she had the attention span of a gnat, and she kept expecting Whittaker to burst through the door any second.

Chase had called several times, but she wasn't about to speak to him. He'd done enough to ruin her career, thank you, and she didn't see the need to help him ruin it further.

After the show, she planned to work on her résumé, although hope of getting another radio show wasn't strong. But she might be able to get a job as a therapist. Not in New York, which was okay. She wouldn't mind moving. She'd find herself a nice college town, perhaps, and settle into private practice. Let the scandal burn itself out. She imagined that, in years to come, her humiliation would lessen, and she'd forget about Chase completely.

Her gaze moved to the computer screen, and she saw the next caller up was Dan from Great Neck. He wanted to talk about his girlfriend and her obsession with a celebrity. Cujo gave her the cue, and she leaned in, forcing herself to think about Dan, to give him her full attention.

"This is Dr. Jamie, and we're talking about sex. Up next is Dan from Great Neck. Dan, you there?"

"Yeah."

"Talk to me."

"I've been seeing this girl for almost a year, and everything's been going pretty well."

"But?"

"But ever since you made that bet, she's been going ape over Chase Newman."

Jamie's gaze darted to the production booth. Marcy had her back turned; she was talking to someone Jamie couldn't see. She'd asked Marcy to shy away from any Chase calls. Had Dan told her the celebrity his girlfriend was obsessed with?

"What do you mean, Dan? How is she going ape?"

He sighed. "She's got about a thousand pictures of the guy from every magazine and newspaper she can find. She and her friends talk about him all the time. I mean it. They don't ever talk about anything else. It's enough to make you sick."

"Now, Dan, infatuations are simply that. A dazzling moment when a person assigns all their wildest dreams to someone they don't know. That person becomes everything good and fine and wonderful, but it's only for a short time. Because it's not real. It can't last. It's an illusion. She'll get over it soon, and when she does, she'll look at you again and wonder how she ever thought Chase Newman could have stolen her heart. You stand by her, let her have her moment, don't belittle her or get angry, and, in the end, she'll see she doesn't have to be dazzled to be happy. She can be herself, with all her flaws, and love you for all that you are."

"Seriously?"

"Yes. Trust me."

"But isn't there a way to get her to stop talking about him so much?"

Jamie opened her mouth, but her thoughts were interrupted by the thick, heavy door swinging open. It wasn't Whittaker; it was Chase. All her higher brain functions stopped, and she was left with a great wallop of fear—and, unbelievably, desire. Her insides were dancing with the duel emotions, and she felt completely helpless. Somewhere in the back of her mind she knew she was supposed to be doing something. But she was frozen, panicked. This was it. He was going to tell the world who she was and what she'd done. From this moment on, her whole life would change. Everyone would know that she was a fraud, a phony.

Worse than that was the way her nipples hardened and her chest constricted. Adrenaline surged through her, and she wasn't so naive as to blame it on anything but the truth. She was infatuated with Chase, just the way Dan's girlfriend was. Only, Jamie's problem was infinitely worse. The man held her future in the palm of his hand. She was in so much trouble.

Chase threw her a maddeningly casual smile as he sat down in front of the nearest guest mike, put on a set of headphones, grinned broadly at Cujo—who grinned back—and pressed the button that would put him on the air.

"Dan?"

"Yeah?"

"This is Chase Newman."

"Oh man. Damn. I didn't mean to—"

"It's all right. Is your girl there?"

"You mean you can't hear her screaming?"

Chase nodded. "When she's done, put her on the phone, okay?"

"Are you kidding? It's bad enough now."

"Trust me."

Chase kept his smile as he looked at Jamie. She wondered which would be more newsworthy—Chase exposing her secret, or her having a seizure on the air. Either way, she wouldn't come out smelling like a rose.

"Hello?" A breathless female, her voice quivering in excitement, came over the airwaves.

"What's your name, darlin'?"

"Oh my God. Marie. My name is Marie. Is it really you?"

"Nice to meet you, Marie. I'm Chase."

A squeal that threatened eardrums all over Manhattan made Jamie jerk her headphones off. Chase winced, but that's all.

"Marie?"

"Oh God."

"Marie, listen up. Jamie was right. I'm not anything special. If you knew me at all, you'd understand that."

"Oh, come on."

He shook his head. "It's true. I'm not any different than Dan. In fact, I'm sure you're better off with him than me."

Jamie put her headphones back on and leaned in to the mike. "Why?" Maybe she could put off the inevitable, at least for a little while. Make this about Chase.

He shifted his gaze to her. "Because I don't share well with others."

"Go on." Jamie kept waiting for the other shoe to drop. Any second now—she could just feel it. Her palms sweated, and she felt a trickle of moisture slither down her back.

"The truth is, Marie, I can be a real son of a bitch."

Jamie closed her eyes, braced for the words that would change everything.

"You?" Marie asked. "I don't believe you."

"You should."

Jamie opened one eye. Chase grinned at her, and she realized he was enjoying her torment. "Believe him," she said into the mike.

"Oh, yeah. Take this bet, for example." He scooted closer to Jamie. "I'm not the least bit worried that I'm going to lose. I've already seduced her. She just doesn't know it yet."

"Is that so?" Jamie moved her chair away from him.

"Honey, it's all there in your eyes." He laughed. "Ladies and gentlemen, the woman wants me. In fact, she wants me so badly she can't keep her hands off me. It's a little embarrassing."

Marie giggled. "So why does that make you a son of a bitch?"

"Because not only am I going to win this bet, but I'm going to win it right now, on the air, with a million witnesses."

Jamie's eyes widened in disbelief as he took hold of the chair arm and pulled her to his side. "Are you nuts?"

"Maybe."

"I think we need to go to commercial."

Chase turned toward the window, toward his buddy Cujo. "I don't think so. We're not leaving until you cry uncle."

Cujo bent to his board, his grin broad and a little wicked.

"Hey," she said, not liking any of this one bit. "This is my show. I say what we do."

"Not tonight," Chase said. He looked at Cujo, who nodded and gave him a thumbs-up. Then Chase's gaze moved back to hers, and that's when she clued in. Blackmail. The bastard was holding her secret for ransom and the payoff was just another form of humiliation.

She punched the mute button and faced him, her fury strong enough to shatter glass. "Stop this right now. If you're going to tell, tell. But I won't be played with like this."

He wiggled his eyebrows in a mock-sexy way. "I like it when you get all fired up."

"Chase, I'm not kidding. I'm not going to let you humiliate me."

"So, you want me to tell your audience about last night?"

"Yes." Her heart nearly stopped beating. "No."

"It's your call."

"You *are* a son of a bitch."

He grinned. "I know."

"You seriously want me to have sex with you here? On the air?"

He nodded as if his request wasn't totally outrageous. To make matters worse, if that were possible, her body didn't seem to grasp the situation at all. In fact, she knew enough about the mechanics to realize that her labia had swelled, that the heat on her chest and below was a triggered response. For all intents and purposes, her body thought this was all foreplay.

He reached over, punched the button on her console that put them back on the air, then moved his hand to the back of her neck. "Welcome back, New York," he whispered, his voice gruff and powerful. Different from the voice of a moment ago. "This is the Dr. Jamie show, and we're not talking anymore."

He pulled her toward him, and while she did protest, it wasn't a world-class effort. Then his lips were on hers, and the war between her mind and her body went ballistic.

She moaned as his tongue slipped between her teeth. He worked his magic, sending shock waves through her veins, right to her most vulnerable parts. Then he pulled back, and the first thing she saw was both his hands. When had he let her go? Why had she felt as if she couldn't pull away?

"Stand up," he said, his voice that intimate whisper that had turned her to mush last night.

Her gaze went to the window. Marcy stood next to Fred, and she was arguing with him. Fred didn't seem to care. Cujo still wore that conspiratorial smile. What was going on? Jamie could see every line was flashing, which reminded her...

"Marie," she said. "Are you still there?"

"Yeah. But don't let me interrupt."

"Jamie has to go now, Marie," Chase said. "But don't turn off your radio." He got up from his chair, went to the wall and turned down the lights, darkening the room just enough so that they could see each other, but the folks in the production booth couldn't.

While Jamie was grateful no one could see, she was acutely aware they could hear. All of Manhattan could hear. This was the moment to bolt. To run out of here, and not stop until she was at her apartment. She could be packed and on a plane in a few hours.

No, wait. Maybe it wasn't so bad. It wasn't as if they were on television. Maybe she could play this to her advantage. She could pretend to go along, and then when Chase was all riled up and thinking he was going to win, she could stop everything. Tell her audience that while Chase was very sexy, she hadn't been seduced, and that she'd proved her point. If she could time it right, she'd be able to end the wager, declare victory and turn off the mike so Chase wouldn't have a chance to spill the beans.

It just might work—if she could keep her cool.

Chase settled back into his chair. "Stand up," he said again, his voice commanding, letting her know exactly how seriously he was taking this.

Saying a quick prayer that she knew what the hell she was doing, she obeyed him. She stood, and he pushed her chair away, then moved his so that she was trapped between him and the desk. He parted his knees and moved closer, boxing her in on all sides.

"Look at me."

She felt her cheeks heat. The awareness that her boss, her producer and God knew who else were standing just a few feet away, listening to the sex in his voice, knowing she was doing as he requested, made her want to disappear. But at the same time, it was sort of exciting—which must mean she was as twisted as Chase.

He touched her knees, and she jumped. His cool hands slipped under her dress and slowly inched up her thighs. "Do you like the feel of my hands on your thighs?"

She looked at him quizzically, wishing the light was a hair brighter so she could study his eyes. Oh damn, he was narrating! Giving the whole world a play-by-play. She couldn't do this. Her show wasn't worth it. Nothing was worth it. She turned to escape, but his hands held her steady.

"Where do you think you're going?"

"Out. I can't do this. I won't do this."

"Look at me."

"No."

"Jamie, look at me."

She slowly turned and met his gaze. She barely registered that he'd taken off his headphones. When had that happened?

"It's going to be fine," he said. "Let yourself go. No one is going to see anything you don't want them to. They'll just hear us—and that's what you do, isn't it? Talk about sex."

"This isn't talk."

"Exactly. It's better than talk." Chase grinned, then leaned toward her mike. "Listen up, all you guys. If you're out there with your girls tonight, join us. Do what we do. Let's make Manhattan into an isle of joy."

"Chase, I can't."

"You can. You are. Just keep looking at me, baby. Just look into my eyes."

The battle continued inside her, but as the seconds ticked by and her heart thudded in her chest, Chase's gaze held her steady. Hypnotized her. Heated her flesh past the edge of comfort.

His hands moved up a few more inches, up to the sides of her underwear. "Hmm. Tell me about your panties, Jamie. What color are they?"

"White."

"They feel like silk."

"I'm not sure what they are."

"They're awfully tiny."

She trembled as his fingers slipped under the elastic and moved inch by inch from her sides to her back. Then his fingers were rubbing at the tender line where her buttocks met the top of her thighs. It was an incredibly intimate gesture. He rubbed her back and forth.

"Jamie."

"Hmm?"

"I want you to lift your dress."

"What?"

"Go on, honey, lift your dress. Let me see those pretty white panties."

She didn't hesitate too long. After all, she'd win in the end. That's what she had to remember. She gathered the material of her dress in her hands and lifted, slowly, slowly, baring her knees, then her thighs. She hesitated just before her panties would have peeked out.

In response, he moved his hands up so that he cupped her buttocks, and he squeezed her flesh. "Higher," he whispered. "Let me see your panties."

Trembling with an excitement she couldn't have acknowledged, she lifted the material the last few inches. He shifted his gaze to what she'd bared, and moaned his pleasure.

"Jamie, you're so beautiful. Those panties are silk, but your skin is softer." He leaned forward and placed a kiss just below her belly button. "And you smell like vanilla and sex."

Marcy had given her vanilla perfume for her birthday, and Jamie had sprayed some on this afternoon after her shower, so that explained half his observation. But did she really smell like sex? It was true that with foreplay, a woman's body would react with lubrication and a very personal, unique scent. Half of what attracted one man to one woman was scent, and there was no telling who would find one odor sexy and another unpleasant.

She leaned slightly forward and breathed deeply. Chase smelled like sex, too. To her, it was intoxicating. Hypnotizing. Dangerous.

He kissed her again, his mouth moving closer to the top of her panties. Squeezing her buttocks again, he traced his tongue down, not even stopping when he hit the silk of her underwear. She held her breath as he kissed her, each kiss slightly below the last.

Just before he reached her mound, he stopped. "Tell them what I'm doing, Jamie."

"I—"

"You can. Just do it. Tell them."

She opened her mouth, but a wave of self-consciousness made her mute. For the first time since she'd been on the radio, sex had made her embarrassed.

"Honey," he whispered, "go on."

Nodding slightly, she closed her eyes, which made things easier. "He's..."

Chase kissed her again on the same spot.

"He's kissing me...over my underwear."

His mouth moved down, getting perilously close to the top of her sex. "Where?" he whispered.

"Near my..."

"What?"

She couldn't. The scientific term was too clinical, the slang expressions too vulgar. There didn't seem to be the right word. Why was that? Why wasn't there a sexy, slightly naughty, erotic word for a woman's genitals?

He chuckled, and then he threw her off another fifty degrees when he blew a stream of warm air right on the lips of her sex. The sensation made her tremble, made her push against his hands, made her want more.

"Tell them, Jamie."

"He's, uh, blowing air—a thin, hot stream of air—on me…"

"That's right. And now what am I doing?"

She gasped. "He's using his fingers. In back."

"How?"

She squeezed her pelvic muscles to stop the sudden ache between her legs. "Oh my God, he's tracing the line of my bottom."

He laughed again. "The line of your bottom?"

"That's as much as you're going to get from me."

His fingers lifted away from her skin. "And what if I were to tell you that's all you'll get from me?"

She pushed back, but he didn't touch her again. His hands were still inside her panties, but there was no contact. The position, however, had another effect, this one on her front. The silk had been pulled tight, forcing the material to slip inside her lips and rub against her.

"Jamie."

"Don't stop," she whispered.

"Then, tell them the truth."

"I will. But the truth isn't about what to call things. The truth is that your touch makes me breathless. That I'm drowning in an ocean of sensation."

"You're being seduced."

"No. Not seduced. Seduced takes all the responsibility away from me. I'm here. I'm moving my hips so the material of my panties can rub exactly the right way. I'm hoping you'll touch me again, that you'll use your hands and your mouth in every way possible to give me pleasure. I'm not being seduced. I'm saying yes. I'm telling you I want you.''

12

CHASE COULD BARELY BREATHE. He'd become so hard that he felt sure one wrong move would cause permanent damage. This level of excitement shocked him. He hadn't known he could feel this way. That he could want someone so badly.

Despite his intention to manipulate the situation, Jamie had managed to take control. That's the thing with women. They could always take control. There were no equal partners when it came to sex. Men were helpless fools the moment the blood rushed south.

What she didn't know was that he'd arranged everything with Cujo. They weren't on the air at all. Cujo was broadcasting the weather and news and whatever else he could come up with until Chase gave him the signal to go back on the air. It was supposed to be his party, his victory. Only, Jamie wasn't surrendering.

"Chase."

"Hmm?"

"Look at me."

He didn't want to. She'd put a spell on him, and he was the one who was helpless now.

"Look at me."

He lifted his gaze. There was just enough light for her gaze to catch his and hold him steady.

"I won't do this," she said, and she let go of her dress. It fluttered on his arms, and he grasped her buttocks again. "No." She reached back and moved his hands, then stepped to the side, escaping from his hold. "You do what you have to do. But I won't play this out, not for you, not for anything. And if that means you need to..." She closed her eyes, unable to say the words, then she looked at him again. "I'll make it easy for you." With that, she put both of her hands on his chest and pushed him back, giving herself an exit. "It's all up to you," she said. Then she took off her headphones, grabbed her purse from beneath the desk and walked to the door.

"Jamie, wait."

She looked back at him, shook her head, and then she was gone.

He stared at the door for a moment, trying to get himself under control. She'd taken him by surprise, turned the tables. He should tell the world what he knew, just to show her who was boss.

Even as the thought entered his head, he realized what a jerk he was. There was no way he was going to hurt her like that. He might be a son of a bitch, but he wasn't a selfish bastard.

This was all supposed to be a laugh. But Jamie had gotten to him. He wasn't sure how. If he'd slept with her, that would explain it—but he hadn't. His physical desire for her wasn't the reason, either.

He cared about what happened to her. And that was something he'd sworn he'd never do.

"Chase?"

He looked up at the speaker mounted on the wall. "What?"

"Chase, what's going on, buddy?"

It was Cujo. He'd forgotten all about him, about the

radio show. Hell, he'd forgotten the rest of the world.
"Let's do it."

"But she's gone."

"I'll take over the rest of the show." He thought
about turning up the lights, but he liked the dark. It
was more suitable for a rat like him. He picked up her
headphones from the desk and put them on. "This is
Chase Newman for Dr. Jamie. And we're talking about
sex."

JAMIE WALKED BLINDLY toward the subway, cursing
herself, cursing Chase, cursing life. By now, he'd un-
doubtedly told the world about her virginity, and the
uproar was probably in full swing. What troubled her
most was that Marcy was finding out this way, instead
of hearing it from Jamie.

How could she have let it get so messed up? My
God, she'd almost made love to him while the whole
world listened in—her mother's friends, her professors,
the men and women she'd gone to school with. If it
had gone any further, she would have had to resign.
Her plan, although desperate, to turn the tables on
Chase had failed, just like every other thing in her life.
No. That wasn't true. She'd done some things right.
She'd found a career she loved. She'd done well aca-
demically. She'd made a true friend in Marcy.

None of her accomplishments felt real, though.
Nothing mattered except Chase and her job. She'd lose
them both tonight, which meant that the only thing
she'd have to hold on to was the fact that she'd gotten
a bunch of *A*s.

Terrific. That should be of great comfort on long,
cold nights as she circled jobs in the want ads.

She veered off her path when she saw a nice bus

stop bench. Even the subway seemed like too much trouble. She'd sit for a few minutes, then she'd take the bus or hail a cab.

Plunking herself down, she sighed as she watched the traffic speed by, the insanity of the driving somehow making sense to her. Even the cacophony of horns and blaring radios and hydraulic brakes seemed appropriate—a fitting sound track to her pathetic life.

Closing her eyes as she leaned her head back, she let herself be swallowed by the noise. It felt good not to think, not to feel, just to hear.

Only, she kept hearing Chase. His voice got louder and louder, and finally her eyes snapped open. She wasn't nuts. A woman had joined her at the bus stop, and she was listening to the radio. Chase was still on the air.

Jamie checked her watch. A good forty-five minutes had passed since she'd run out of the station. She focused on the woman's radio, wanting to hear what he had to say.

"…empty. I'm serious. There's nothing there."

"That's not true," a female caller said. "You wouldn't be there if you didn't care about anything."

"You misunderstood," Chase said, his voice making Jamie ache all over again. "I said I didn't care about *anyone,* not *anything.*"

"Same difference."

"Not true. I can care about racing with all my energy. But if I should stop racing, the cars wouldn't give a damn. That's not how it is with people."

"Are you trying to tell me you don't care about Dr. Jamie?"

Silence. Jamie's heart stopped, and she crossed her fingers.

"That's right," Chase said finally. His voice was weary and despondent, but the message was clear as crystal. "I'm not saying she's not great—she is. I'm just not the kind of guy who can love her."

"There's a kind of guy?"

"Sure. You know that. You see them going to work every day, picking up milk at the store. They're the guys at the baseball fields in the summer, watching their kids learn to hit the ball. They're in it for the long haul."

"And you're not?"

"No."

"Why not?"

Silence once again, but Jamie didn't care this time. She had heard all she needed to. His confession had made something very evident—she'd wanted him to want her and not just for sex. Even though she hadn't been aware of her desire, her disappointment underscored how deeply she'd felt.

"I don't stick around," Chase said, "not for anyone."

"Aren't you afraid you're going to end up old and alone?"

"No," he said, and there was something about his voice that made her strain to hear the next words. "I'm not afraid of that at all."

CHASE SLUMPED in the elevator, wrung out from the night. Somehow he'd managed to finish Jamie's show. But that wasn't what had him in knots.

Damn that Fred Holt. The show had never gone off the air. Cujo had given the signal, but Fred had put the kibosh on the plan, and no one had bothered to tell

Chase. So all that seduction, all that intimate talk had gone out to a little over a million homes. Great.

If only she'd answered her phone, called him back. He never would have cooked up this crazy scheme.

It had all gone to hell in a hand basket. Instead of the playful teasing he'd hoped would make her realize he had no intention of blowing the whistle on her, things had spun completely out of control.

For a man with a huge ego, he sure did seem to have a talent for public humiliation. Not Jamie's. His own. Shit, how was he going to convince her that he'd never meant that stuff to be on the air? And that he would never tell anyone her secret.

He had to figure out a way to lose the bet without making himself the laughingstock of New York. If he couldn't, then he deserved what he got.

All he wanted in the immediate future, however, was to go to bed and sleep for about fifteen hours. Damn, but he could almost feel the cool, crisp hotel sheets calling him.

The elevator came to a stop on the ground floor, and the doors slid open. He walked across the lobby, nodding to the night watchman. The heat outside hit him hard. He hated summers in Manhattan. Better to be on the west coast this time of year—San Diego or San Francisco.

He stopped short when he saw Rupert Davidson leaning against a spit-shined Cadillac. This wasn't good. Rupert was never up this late.

Chase headed toward his manager, his heart beating fast.

"Chase."

"What's wrong?"

"You have a minute?"

"Rupert, what is it? Is my mother all right?"

The older man nodded. "Yes. No one's ill. I just want to talk to you."

"Fine."

Rupert opened the passenger door, and Chase got in. Once Rupert was inside, the driver took off, not asking where they were going. He already must have known.

"What's going on?"

"I heard your radio show tonight."

"Yeah?"

"All of it."

Chase's defenses went up immediately, although he stopped himself from justifying his actions. He wanted to hear this through.

After a few moments of stony silence, Rupert nodded, cleared his throat and went on. "Your mother heard it, too. She called me. Chase, she was crying."

"Why?"

"Because she hates what you're doing with your life. She feels like she failed you."

"Hey, it was a joke. I wasn't really going to have sex on the air."

"That's not the part that bothered her, although she wasn't thrilled."

"What do you mean?"

"You said some things tonight about not caring, about never sticking around."

"So?"

"So, she wept bitter tears that she'd raised a son with such a narrow vision of life."

Chase inched closer to the door. "You know, of all the people in the world who should understand—"

"Understand what?"

"Why I won't let myself care. Jeez, she was a basket

case for years after Dad died. She could hardly function."

"So?"

"Why would I want to do that to someone?"

Rupert sighed. "You're not going to die at thirty-five, Chase."

"How the hell do you know?"

"I just do." Rupert looked him over, then shook his head. "I suppose I should tell you. I've asked your mother to marry me. She's graciously agreed."

The news hit him like a slap. Rupert had finally proposed. Why should it surprise him? He'd been suggesting the very thing for years now. Only, somehow, he never expected... "That's great, Rupert. I mean it. You two should be together."

"Chase, let me ask you something."

"What?" He turned to the window.

"What if—and don't jump all over me—what if you didn't know you were going to die? What would you do differently?"

Chase stared at a billboard with a semi-naked woman swooning over eye shadow. What would he do differently? "I don't know."

"Yes, you do."

He did. He just didn't want to think about it. Because then he'd have to think about everything he'd missed for all these years. Everything he was missing now. Jamie. Loving her. Not fighting his feelings. Watching the seasons go by with her by his side. Children. Dammit, he'd do it *all* differently—but the fact was, he had no future. Sure, he could care about her and be glad of every day. But what about her, after he was gone? What kind of a schmuck would he be to let her love him when he had so little time left?

"I can't tell you what to do," Rupert said, his voice low, tired. "But you don't have to wait until thirty-five to die. You're already dead. By your own hand. You've kept yourself apart from everyone, made yourself an island. That's not what God intended for us, Chase. You have a right to live fully. To love. To care."

Chase leaned forward and tapped the driver on the shoulder. "Pull over."

The driver looked up and checked with Rupert, who nodded. Then they were at the curb, and Chase finally faced his friend. "I miss my father every day," he said.

"Would it be better never to have known him?"

"Maybe."

"Then, I'm sorry for you."

Chase stepped out on the street. He watched the black car disappear into traffic. Rupert had meant well. He just didn't understand. Neither did his mother, which was harder to accept. How many times had she told him that his father was a bastard for dying? That she hated him for leaving?

Chase had learned a lot from his father's death. He understood where his responsibilities lay. But, for the first time ever, he wished things were different. He wished he didn't have to go. He wished he could be like all the other slobs out there, not having a clue when the end was going to come. It was the not knowing that made it possible to love. That underlying awareness of mortality.

But Chase knew what was in store. The goal was to leave with the fewest people getting hurt.

He turned toward home and walked into the shadows of the night.

JAMIE LISTENED to Marcy's message twice, but there was no hint that Chase had told her secret. She felt relieved, but not much better. The ache in her chest, planted last night by Chase's brutal admissions, had ruined her sleep.

It wasn't his fault, but her own. She was the one who'd been acting like a fool, who'd taken a stupid publicity stunt and twisted it into something it wasn't. He owed her nothing. She had no business wanting him.

But she did.

And that was about the saddest thing she could think of. Never before had she let herself care about a man. Oh, sure, there was family love, but this was something completely different. This was the kind of romantic attraction she'd read about in her beloved books, from *Pride and Prejudice* to *Gone with the Wind*. Or perhaps it would be more accurate to compare it to a Stephen King novel.

She might still be a virgin, but she was well and truly screwed.

The most horrible part was that Chase had been her last thought before sleep, and her first thought upon awaking. He'd made her dreams wicked and hot, and her body so sensitive that she'd been constantly aroused.

One good thing, if she survived this, was that she understood so much more now. While she didn't regret the basic advice she'd given her listeners in college or more recently, she would have worded things differently. Couched her phrases with more compassion, tried to be more sympathetic.

She'd always known there was such a thing as intuitive knowledge that had very little to do with intellectual knowledge. But she'd always believed that the intellectual was stronger. Now, she wasn't so sure. Despite knowing the truth about her nonexistent relationship with Chase, she continued to want him, to dream of him.

So what did that say about seduction? Was it possible seduction was just the intuitive brain taking over? Was it really not weakness or a wish to give up responsibility?

If that was the case, then she had a lot of apologizing to do. She wasn't quite ready to take a stand one way or the other. All she knew was that last night she'd wanted to make love to Chase, but that she'd stopped before things had gone beyond the point of no return. It had taken all her strength, but she'd done it.

Would she have been able to do the same if they'd been alone? Who knows? Maybe not. And if she had succumbed, would she have been strong enough to accept her own responsibility in the matter?

Sighing heavily, she poured herself another cup of coffee, then sat down at the dining room table. It was her day off, and aside from the nap she so desperately needed, she also had some errands to run. Groceries. The dry cleaner. And perhaps a trip to her favorite secondhand store.

Keeping busy was a good idea. Now, all she had to do was build up enough energy to get dressed.

Another sip, and she was on her feet. But she didn't make it to her bedroom. A knock on the door jumpstarted her pulse, and she spilled her coffee all over the floor.

She moved slowly toward the door, not at all sure what to do. Let him in? Tell him to leave? Cry? She rose on tiptoe and peeked through the little hole. It wasn't Chase. It was worse.

She unlocked the door and swung it open. "Hello, Mother."

"Jamie."

Her mother, dressed in her usual impeccable suit—blue with a white, starched blouse, navy flats, and a handbag to match—walked past her into the apartment. Jamie knew this confrontation was inevitable, but she'd hoped to have it over the phone.

She shut the door behind her. "How are you?"

"I'm fine, so is your father. Although this radio—"

"Want some coffee?" Jamie asked, cutting her off. She wasn't ready yet.

Her mother looked her up and down, and she wished she'd put on her robe. Her nightgown had a tear on the shoulder. "Sit down, Jamie. We need to talk."

She obeyed. Because she always obeyed. She didn't want to talk to her mother. Didn't want to hear the lecture, to see the look of disappointment on her face. It wasn't as if Jamie didn't know she was making a spectacle of herself.

"Your father and I are concerned over this radio business."

"I know."

"Do you also know that you're becoming a laughingstock? That my friends have started to makes jokes about you?"

"It's my job, Mother."

"It's not a job. It's a disgrace. You're a PhD, Jamie, and you're throwing your education down the drain. How do you expect to be an equal among your peers? I see you on the side of buses, on billboards, along with that horrible man. What's gotten into you? I thought we'd raised you better than this."

Jamie's gut clenched, and an anger she'd rarely felt

bubbled up from somewhere deep inside. "Mother, how old am I?"

"You're twenty-six. What kind of a question is—"

"And when you were twenty-six, you had already married Dad and you were pregnant with Kyle."

"What's your point?"

"I'm a grown woman and what I do is none of your business."

"That's where you're wrong. People know I'm your mother. People assume it's your upbringing that's led you to these ridiculous stunts. How do you think that makes me feel?"

"You know what?" She stood. "I don't care. You'll just have to find a way to cope. If I embarrass you so much, just lie. Tell people that I've gone mad, that I'm adopted—whatever you like."

"Jamie—"

"I'm in the middle of the worst crisis of my life, and all you can think about is your reputation. I've always done what you said. Until you wanted me to give up the one thing that's totally mine. I love my show, and I love being on the radio. And if I have to do this stupid stunt to keep my show, then I'm willing. This is mine, Mother, all mine. And nothing you can say will change that."

"I see." Her mother rose and picked up her purse. "I was going to make you an offer. Your father and I had wanted you to join us in our practice. But I can see we were once again being too generous. You don't want our help."

"I just want your love, unconditionally. Whether you think I'm being a damn fool or not."

"Love is earned, Jamie."

"No, it's not. Respect is earned. Love is given, freely, no strings."

"Do you respect him? When he lifted your dress up while you were on the air, was it respect you felt?"

"It's complicated."

Her mother nodded. "Think about what you're do-ing. What this escapade is going to mean to your fu-ture. Don't throw it all away, Jamie. You're bright. You can have a great practice. But you can't have it all. Either you're a disk jockey or you're a doctor."

Jamie nodded, even though she disagreed. Nothing she was going to say would change her mother. And if she expected unconditional love from her mother, wasn't it only just that she give the same thing? That she accept her mother for all she was, the good and the bad?

"Mom," she said, as they walked to the door. "I know you want the best for me. And I appreciate that."

"You do?"

"Yes." She kissed the pale cheek, and the scent of lilacs spun her into childhood for a moment. Her mother had always smelled like lilacs. "I love you."

Her mother shook her head, then looked her straight in the eye. "I love you, too, even though you seem to delight in making that difficult."

"Say hi to Dad, okay?"

A wan smile, and then Jamie closed the door. She had no desire to hurt her parents. But she was way past living the life they wanted for her.

This was her crisis, dammit, all of her own making. And it signaled, in a very large way, that she had finally become a woman. She'd slipped out from under her parents' control. How ironic.

13

MARCY HEARD Ted's voice, but she wasn't certain where he was. Probably behind the big file cabinet, just out of her line of sight. She touched her hair, moistened her lips. Tonight was dinner, their first real date. She couldn't have been more excited. In fact, it was only after she'd been at the station for about an hour that she noticed she'd worn one black pump and one navy. Lucky for her, she'd been able to scoot home and change before anyone else had seen.

Laughter. Ted's rich baritone. And she heard Cal, the morning commute DJ and the biggest gossip since Hedda Hopper. Why Cal was here this time of night, Marcy couldn't fathom, but who could figure out radio personalities. They were all nuts—except Ted, of course. He was perfect.

She listened as she headed around the cabinet, trying to determine if the conversation was private or if she could butt in.

"…a good kid," Ted said.

"Yeah. But between you, me and the lamppost, if I wasn't already married…"

"You old scoundrel."

"That's about the nicest thing anyone's ever called me. What I don't get is why you're not all over her."

"I don't know how smart it is to get involved with someone at work."

Marcy froze. She shouldn't be hearing this. Were they talking about her? Was she the "good kid"? Or maybe it was Jamie. Please let it be about Jamie.

"With those long legs? Are you kidding me? Besides, I heard a rumor that she's been checking you out."

"That's probably because we're going to dinner tonight. But it's not a date, just a friendly meal."

"Friendly meals can sometimes turn into something better."

"That's not going to happen," Ted said. "I'm not interested in her in that way."

Marcy leaned her head against the wall and closed her eyes. She was such a dope. How could she ever have thought Ted would be interested in her. She was so much older. He could have anyone he wanted. Dammit, why had she asked him out?

"I'm going to get some coffee," Ted said. "You want some?"

"Nope. I'm going home. Get myself something decent to drink."

Marcy darted down the hallway and ducked into the first door she saw. It was, unfortunately, the storage closet, and in order to shut the door behind her she had to squash herself between a cleaning cart and several cases of computer paper. Once safely hidden in the dark space, she had plenty of time to think about her folly. She should have known better. Why did she always have to do this to herself? She wasn't unhappy. So what if she was single? This was the twenty-first century, for heaven's sake. Who said she had to be married?

Of course, she didn't honestly think one date with Ted would automatically lead to marriage. Although, dammit, she'd entertained the notion. It would have been nice, really nice. Ted was a decent guy, one of the nicest men she'd ever met. He'd just proved himself by not talking about her lasciviously with Cal when the opportunity presented itself. She should be grateful about that.

But she didn't feel grateful. All she felt was exhausted. She wanted to go home. To crawl into bed and stay there for about two weeks. Instead, she had to go man the phones. If the ratings stayed consistent, tonight should be a killer.

Work would help. It would. She just had to stop thinking about the things she couldn't have. Her life worked, and it would continue to work long after Ted Kagan was a vague memory.

"JAMIE, IT'S CHASE."

The words hung in the air in the broadcast booth. Marcy stared at her worriedly, but Jamie just smiled, nodded and hit the button that would connect Chase to her and her audience.

"We have an old friend here," she said, amazed that she sounded so calm, so together. Her insides were doing a tango, and she had to sip some water to wet her suddenly dry mouth. "Hello, Chase."

"You didn't call me back," he said.

Just hearing him started the complex series of bodily reactions she'd given up trying to understand. He changed her, that's all. Altered who she was and what she felt. Her guess was that it happened in her chromosomes, and that it was, in essence, magic. "We're talking now."

"I thought we might do it a little more privately."

"Why? We've done everything else on the air."

He was quiet for a moment, and she wished she hadn't said that. She should have called him back. But talking to him solo wasn't in her best interest. She'd thought about it for two long days, then decided against it. She'd cry, and she didn't want him to see that. She might do a lot of things she'd regret. This was safer.

"All right. We'll do it your way."

"It's the way we both agreed to do it," she reminded him. "You knew from the start this was going to be public."

"Right. You're right. So, I guess I'll just say it. I give. You won."

"Pardon?"

"I said, I quit. I didn't seduce you. And I know that it's useless to keep on trying. You're right about all of it. No one can be seduced without their permission."

"But—"

"I just wanted your listeners to know, and I won't have another chance to tell them. I'm leaving. I'm going to Paris in a couple of days, then to Budapest."

"You're leaving?"

"Yeah. I wanted to tell you yesterday, but—"

"But I didn't return your call."

"Right."

Jamie refused to cry, even though her eyes filled with hot tears. His respect for her made everything worse. Not only had he kept her secret, but he'd lied about not seducing her—because even though they hadn't had sex, he *had* successfully seduced her. She'd grown used to the idea that he was a selfish son of a bitch—and then he'd gone and done this.

"So, uh, I guess that's all, huh?"

"No. It's not all. It can't be."

"Why?"

"Because..." She tried to think of something that would keep him here, or, if not that, some way to say thanks. "Because there was no default clause. The deal was for two weeks. How do you know you wouldn't be able to seduce me tomorrow? Or in two days?"

"Ah, Jamie," he said, his voice so full of sadness and futility. "Babe, you know that it's not meant to be, right?"

He wasn't talking about the stupid bet. He was talking about them, about a future. Of course she knew it wasn't meant to be. Why would it? Just because he turned her on? Because her stomach did flip-flops whenever he was around? That wasn't love. It was lust. The very thing she told her listeners to watch out for.

"Anyway, I've, uh, got to—"

"Don't," she said, her hand going to the small speaker on her console. "Please."

"It's been fun. I mean it. You're a class act, Jamie, and New York is lucky to have you."

She heard the *click* of his phone, and then in an act of mercy, Cujo took it away to play the news and weather.

"You okay?" asked Marcy over the speaker.

She looked at Marcy in the other room and she nodded, even though she wasn't okay. Far from it. She felt more like a fraud than ever. Chase had been the class act, not her. He'd been willing to make a fool of himself for her, and he'd done it in the most public way.

She hadn't anticipated that he might just up and leave. Not so soon. Not before they—

"Oh God." The words slipped out as she came to grips with the realization that she wanted to sleep with Chase. No, not that she wanted to, but that she'd assumed she would. He was supposed to be the first guy. The one she'd remember forever.

It wasn't possible, not really. She couldn't...

Was that why she'd let him discover the truth about her? Because all along she'd wanted him to be the one? Because...she was falling in love?

Talk about being a hypocrite. She wanted to have sex with him, and she was totally prepared to blame her actions on him. Even after all her degrees, she hadn't seen her own motivation, her own manipulation. She was great when it came to essay questions, but she sucked in the lab. Real life wasn't like the books; it wasn't so black and white.

It didn't matter. Who cared about a stupid bet? Let Whittaker write whatever she wanted. The lesson here was a whopper. She had no business telling people what to do with their lives. None at all.

She caught Cujo's hand signal out of the corner of her eye. The show would go on, at least for tonight. Tomorrow, she would tender her resignation.

CHASE LOOKED at the phone, wondering what he would say if it was Jamie. Who else would be calling? He didn't want to talk to her now, not while he was so busy wallowing in self-pity.

He lifted the phone on the seventh ring, knowing it was a mistake. "Hello."

"What's going on, Chase?"

It wasn't Jamie. "Who is this?"

"Darlene Whittaker. I just heard your noble little speech, and I want to know what's going on."

"If you heard me, then you know. I lost."

"Bull."

"Are you calling me a liar?"

"Yeah. I don't know what went on with you two, but I'll be damned if I believe you couldn't get to her."

"I couldn't."

"A friend of mine saw you two together the other night. According to him, you both looked like you couldn't wait to get to your room. What was that about?"

"Spying on us? Very ethical."

"I didn't send him there to spy. He just happened to see you. So what gives? There's something fishy going on here, and I want to know what it is."

"Darlene, let it go. You have your story. I'm out of here. The end."

"Come on, Chase. I need this. I heard all kinds of rumors about her. Like, for example, that she's not who she claims to be. Her college roommate swore up and down that she never had a date. That she's gay or celibate or both."

"I can't help you."

"You won't."

"Okay."

"I can get the magazine to pay you."

"I don't need money."

"What do you need? I'll get it."

"What is it with you? Why do you want this so badly? What did Jamie ever do to you?"

Darlene was silent for a moment. "I don't like to be snowed, Chase, and neither does the American public."

"Oh, so this is a patriotic effort?"

"A fraud is a fraud is a fraud. Just because she's pretty, she thinks she can get away with anything. God, she's just like the girls I went to school with. As if they're entitled to get everything they want without having to work for it. As if the rest of us should walk ten steps behind—''

''Darlene,'' Chase said, ''this isn't about Jamie. Get help.'' He hung up, then sat down on the couch. Something clicked about what Darlene had said. That stuff about Jamie's college roommate.

Great. He'd been played like a violin by a woman he didn't even know. She'd set him up, but he'd run with it, and if things had gone Darlene's way, he could have destroyed Jamie's career. All for the sake of his masculine pride.

He didn't feel proud now. In fact, he felt like crap. Leaving was a good idea. He'd go to Paris, get back into his car, get ready for Budapest. That would keep him from thinking about Jamie. About the mess he'd made.

It was odd. He'd left a lot of women in his life. It never ruffled his feathers—even if the sex had been great and the connection strong. But leaving Jamie wasn't like that. He felt strange, conflicted. Probably because he hadn't slept with her. Because she was still a mystery to him.

And because he liked her eyes. The little smile she wore when she listened to him. The way she smelled. The way her hair always looked as if she'd run her fingers through it.

He closed his eyes. Tomorrow he would make his reservations. Make sure his team got packed and moving. But for tonight, all he wanted to do was sleep. His head lolled back against the overstuffed chair.

He thought about Jamie as he drifted away.

HE JERKED AWAKE, disoriented. Unsure of the time, the day, of anything, he pulled it together enough to realize the banging he heard was coming from the door.

Hauling himself up, he glanced at his watch as he went to see who the hell it was. Three-thirty in the morning? Shit.

Pulling the door open, his tirade stopped before it began. Jamie stood in the hallway, her pale skin making her dark eyes seem huge.

"You were sleeping, weren't you."

He nodded.

"I'm sorry. Go on back to bed."

She turned, but he caught her before she got too far. "Hold it."

"No, I shouldn't have come. I'm sorry."

"Jamie, I'm too tired to argue. Just come inside."

She paused and looked at him, then she walked into his suite. She had on a skirt and a blouse, and for once the outfit wasn't several sizes too big. It was particularly nice from the back, the way the skirt hugged her derriere. His libido stirred even before he was fully awake.

"I've been downstairs for an hour," she said, not looking at him, but instead staring out the window.

"Why didn't you come up?"

"Because I'm a big, fat coward."

He smiled. "Hold that thought." Picking up the phone, he dialed room service and ordered a pot of coffee and a bottle of vodka. One would wake him up, the other put him to sleep. He didn't know yet which one he'd need. After the call, he walked over to where Jamie stood. "So talk to me."

"I don't know how."

"Yes, you do. You're a great talker. All of New York knows that."

Her head came up and her gaze met his. "You're

right. I'm a hell of a talker. Unfortunately, I don't know what the hell I'm talking about."

"Jamie—"

"I'm quitting."

"What?"

"I'm turning in my resignation tomorrow. I can't do this. I can't continue to lie like this."

"Lie? You haven't lied. Jamie, you're good at what you do. Damn good. Why throw it away over something stupid like this?"

"Because it isn't stupid. I'm a fraud, and you know it."

"Do you think things would be so different if you'd slept with someone?"

She nodded. "I do."

"You're wrong. Sex doesn't change much of anything. It takes the edge off, but that's about it."

"I can't believe you feel that way."

He shrugged. "It's the truth."

"No. That much I do know. Making love changes everything...if it's with the right person."

He was the one to turn to the window this time. "I don't know about that."

"Chase?"

"Hmm?"

"I didn't come up here to tell you I was quitting."

Something about her voice made him look at her. "Yeah?"

"I came up here to ask you to do me a favor."

He knew what she was going to say. And his whole body prepared to answer her.

"I want to make love to you. Tonight. Now."

He wanted to pick her up and throw her on the bed

without another word, but he held himself steady. "I don't think that would be very smart."

She winced, then turned sharply toward the door.

Again, he caught her arm. "Jamie, stop."

She shook her head. "Just let me go. I'm sorry. I shouldn't have asked—"

"Hey. I didn't say I didn't want to."

She stopped tugging, trying to get away. "You didn't?"

"Look at me."

She turned, her cheeks flushed with pink.

"Why?" he asked. "Why do you want to sleep with me?"

"I don't," she said. "I want to make love."

He nodded, somewhat impatient.

She took in a deep breath, let it out slowly. Her gaze steadied, and she faced him squarely. "I want you."

"Why?"

"I don't know. But I do know that every time I hear your voice, I melt. When I'm with you, I feel dizzy and lighter than air. Touching you makes me quiver, and kissing you…" She hid her face behind her hands.

Damn if she wasn't the most adorable creature in the history of the world. "Jamie."

She shook her head, not daring to look at him through her fingers.

He pulled her into his arms, and she snuggled against him. Her heart beat so hard, he could feel it. Her heat warmed him and her scent made him crazy. He kissed the top of her head, and then he leaned down to her ear.

"Me, too," he whispered.

"Really?" Her voice was muffled and tiny, and it made him ache for her.

He put his hands on her shoulders and pushed her back, not away, but so he could see her face. Of course, she was still hiding behind her fingers, but a moment later she dropped her hands. "Really?" she asked again.

He nodded. "I don't want to hurt you."

"You won't."

"You can't know that."

"Let me be responsible for myself," she said. "I'm tired of letting other people make my decisions for me. If you want to make love to me, great. If you don't, I'll get over it. But do whatever because of you, not me."

"See?"

She tilted her head. "What?"

"You can't quit the show. The world needs to hear from you. Your listeners need to hear that."

She smiled, and he felt as if he'd just gotten a great present. Then she rose on her tiptoes, took his cheeks in both her hands and kissed him on the lips. Softly.

Something incredible was about to happen.

14

JAMIE KNEW the exact second he changed his mind. It was all in his kiss, from tentative to bold, from passive to aggressive, from friends to lovers.

His arms went around her as his tongue parted her lips. She wanted to hurry to the bed, but then she would have missed the way his hands moved over her back, down the contours of her hips. She wanted it all, to drown in his arms, to do it all now, even as he took his time.

His lips moved from hers and he nibbled her neck, just below her ear. Goose bumps popped out all over her arms, and she quivered like a bow string. He knew so much, and she knew so little.

No, that wasn't true. She'd read about this over and over again. She'd studied the techniques, and all she had to do was put them to practice.

Kissing. What did she know about kissing? Men liked to mimic sex, to thrust boldly, a prelude, a living illustration. But they also liked to show how they understood a woman's body. Okay, that's why he was nipping her earlobe. She moaned, letting him know he was doing just fine.

Her thoughts sped ahead to the bedroom. Men are visual. She should undress slowly. Tease him. Make him grow hard watching her.

Actually, that last part wasn't going to be very difficult. She could feel him as she pressed against him. He was already hard. So, what was he waiting for?

Reaching behind, she caught his hands, then pulled away from his kisses. "Come with me," she whispered. She led him past the couch and the TV console into the bedroom. He hadn't disturbed his sheets—yet.

She steered him to the bed and pushed on his shoulders till he sat down. "Wait," she said, trying to think of every seductive trick she'd ever read. She moved back so he could see her whole body, but not too far, because men liked the details. Music. Shouldn't there be music? No. Unnecessary. Think visual. Men like to look.

She stood in front of him and took hold of the bottom of her blouse. Lifting slowly, forcing herself to keep a pace that just about killed her, she bared her tummy, and then the bottom of her bra—which, dammit, was just white, boring and utilitarian, but she hadn't known this afternoon that she was going to sleep with him tonight. It was okay, though. Because men didn't care what kind of underwear women wore, just so long as it was intimate apparel.

She wondered if she should move her hips, even though there was no music. Kim Basinger did that wild striptease for Mickey Rourke in *Nine and a Half Weeks*. But that movie had a score, and Jamie's life didn't.

No, she wouldn't move. Well, she'd move a little. The blouse cleared her breasts and then moved up to her neck. As she lifted farther, the material blocked her view of Chase. Wait. Hold it. She was choking herself. Screw the pace, she had to take the damn shirt off.

Once it had cleared her head, she smiled as seductively as she could and tossed the blouse behind her.

A *thud* on wood reminded her that while tossing clothes was sexy, breaking things was not.

"Jamie—"

"Wait. I'm not done." She went to the back of her skirt and lowered her zipper. Too fast. And she was supposed to let him see her do that. She pulled the zipper up and turned around, then slowly pulled it down once more.

She looked at him over her shoulder. Emotions washed over his face, and his cheeks filled with heat. It was working. Maybe she would give him a little of the old bump and grind. Why not?

She thrust her hips out to the right, then turned her head the other way and pushed her hips to the left. Oh, great. Now all she could think of was the Hokeypokey.

She focused on the task at hand. She was driving him crazy with lust, and she couldn't stop now. The zipper finally came to a stop, and then she hooked her thumbs under the waistband.

Down went her skirt, and after she got it past her hips, she turned to face him again. He was still on the pink side. And he looked as if he was struggling not to take her on the spot.

Bless her textbooks. Bless Nancy Friday and Masters and Johnson and *Yellow Silk.* She let her skirt drop, and just as she was stepping out of it, there was a loud knock on the door that scared her half to death. She dove for cover, and her foot got caught in her skirt. Flailing her arms like two propellers, she managed to keep herself upright, barely. It was Chase who steadied her.

Luckily, he went to the door while she gathered her composure. She'd forgotten about room service. But that was okay. She hadn't gotten to the nitty-gritty of her striptease yet.

While he was gone, she could also retrieve her blouse and skirt. No need for them to be wrinkled. The shirt was on his dresser, and she'd knocked over his cologne bottle. Nothing had spilled, though. Checking to make sure he was still busy, she opened the purple bottle and sniffed. The scent was rich and spicy and masculine, just like Chase. She remembered a hint of it on his skin, a suggestion of something forbidden.

She put it down the second she heard him at the bedroom door. Whirling around, she smiled, preparing herself for Act II.

"Jamie—"

"Wait. Sit down."

"But—"

"Please. I don't want to lose my nerve."

He hesitated, then nodded as he went to his former position on the bed. But the pink had left his cheeks and his expression had become rather stoic. She had her work cut out for her.

Hurrying to center stage, she reached back to unhook her bra. By the second loop she remembered to smile. Of course, she didn't just let the bra fall. Her arms, clamped to her sides, held it on. Seductively and bit by bit, she slipped the first bra strap off her shoulder, then the second.

All that was left was the boob portion. Oh, my. The lights were very bright. But it was Chase, and she wanted him to know everything about her, didn't she?

She lifted her arms and the bra landed at her feet. Chase went into a coughing fit, and she tried to remember if she'd ever read about coughing and libido.

Probably. He had to turn away for a moment while he gathered himself together, but she didn't mind the wait.

Looking down, she saw her nipples were hard as erasers and standing out kind of far. Would he like them? She didn't sag very much, but her boobs weren't going to win any prizes. They were just…boobs.

Anyway, Chase had calmed down and he was looking at her again. It was time for Act III. The panties.

She'd picked a standard pair of blue bikinis this morning, not knowing, of course, that she'd be taking them off so publicly. At least they had no holes.

Thumbs under the waistband, then push down. Slower. This was it, he was going to see her completely naked. He'd be the first man. How she'd dreamed of this moment. But in her dreams, the lights weren't quite so bright.

She felt her own cheeks heat as she pushed her panties down over her butt, and then they were around her thighs, and she just wanted them off so she could get to the bed and climb under the covers. *He* might be visually stimulated, but *she* felt like a fool.

Yeah, yeah, it was all natural and wonderful, and part of the life cycle and all that crap, but she was standing in front of Chase Newman, who was fully clothed, while she was stark naked.

She should turn around. She didn't want to, but he would like it. Okay. Smile. Turn.

When she'd finished the one-hundred-eighty degree turn, the red had come back to Chase's face, and he looked as if he was going to have another coughing fit. Maybe he wasn't feeling well.

She approached him, trying to walk sexy but growing concerned. "Chase? Are you sick?"

He shook his head, then turned to the side.

This wasn't amusing. Now she was worried. She moved to the side of the bed and sat down. "Chase, look at me."

He shook his head again.

Since he wouldn't move, she did. When she was on the other side of him, he tried to hide his face, but she wouldn't let him. She wasn't an MD but she would know if he needed to see someone for his cough.

She tugged at his hands, and they came away from his mouth. His eyes were red-rimmed, and his whole face was hot. This was looking serious, and she was just about to suggest they go to the emergency room when a sound burst out of Chase. Not a cough. A laugh.

Ohmygod, he wasn't choking. He was laughing. She bolted off the bed, grabbed a pillow and put it in front of her nakedness.

He let loose with a snort and shook his head, trying like hell to wipe the grin from his face, but it was too late. Her humiliation was total, and all she wanted to do was get the hell out of Dodge.

She moved toward her skirt—the heck with her underpants. Out. She needed to get out.

"Jamie—"

"Please don't say anything," she begged. "I can't take it. I'm sorry. I'm so sorry."

His laughter subsided suddenly, as if a light switch had been turned off. He stood, headed toward her, and if she wasn't fast, he'd be between her and her clothes.

"Honey, don't."

"I asked you not to say anything."

"I have to." He planted himself in front of her, blocking her clothes and her exit. "Please, don't go. I wasn't laughing at you."

"Right. You were just laughing near me. Go away."

He cupped her cheek with his palm. "I don't think I've ever wanted to be with anyone more than I want to be with you right now."

She winced. "Pinocchio, your nose is getting longer."

His low chuckle made her open her eyes. "You're really bad at anatomy."

Her gaze shot down to his pants, and, sure enough, there was a nice-size bulge right where it should be. "Don't tell me you have a fetish for inept strippers."

"I don't. But I think I've got a problem with beautiful radio talk-show hosts."

"Barbara DeAngelis will be glad to hear it."

"Jamie, honey, stop. I think you're wonderful, and delicious, and I loved what you did, and I think I was laughing out of sheer pleasure. You're completely unexpected, you know that?"

"Is that a good thing?"

"Yeah. It's a good thing."

"So there was nothing about my body that put you into hysterics?"

"No." His hand moved from her cheek to the pillow, and he lifted it out of her arms. "You're exquisite. In every detail."

"You don't have to go overboard."

"Would you cut it out? I don't lie."

The joke was over. "Yes, you do. You lied for me on the radio."

"I did not. I didn't seduce you. You won."

"You and I both know that's not true. You seduced me, all right. You made my knees weak and my heart pound, to say nothing of what happened to the, uh, other parts."

His smile turned mischievous. "Is that so?"

She nodded.

"Now, what parts would those be?" He touched her shoulder with the pad of his index finger. "Here?"

She shook her head.

Looking puzzled, he moved the finger to the tip of her nose.

"You're ice cold."

"Hmm." His finger moved to the space between her breasts, and he let it trail slowly downward.

"Warmer," she whispered, and the word described her, too.

Then, looking into her eyes as if she held magic, he circled her breast over and over, the circles becoming smaller and smaller until he was almost touching her nipple. Then his other hand got busy, and, before she even had time to think, she was aching in a way that had everything to do with Chase and being a woman. She was ready.

Her eyes fluttered closed the second he touched her swollen buds. The sensation was unbelievable. Intimate, stirring, thrilling. But, being very greedy, she wanted more.

It didn't seem at all weird to let her hand drift to his pants, to the straining hardness beneath the denim. His moan made her braver, and she found his belt buckle.

Despite her awkward struggles, she got the belt undone, then concentrated on the buttons of his fly, which turned out to be trickier, probably because there was so much strain on the material. He ended up helping her, which didn't matter at all. In fact, he unceremoniously yanked his pants down, then tossed them away, and there he was, in his boxers and his socks. The socks held no interest. The boxers, plenty.

His erection pressed the material out in a tent worthy of an Eagle scout. She had to accept the proof that his laughter wasn't a sign of disinterest. Far from it.

She reached a tentative hand to the front of his shorts and cupped her palm around the bulge. He inhaled sharply, and she felt his penis jerk.

Her previous embarrassment forgotten, she thought of nothing but his body, her body, and what they were about to do. Twenty-six years she'd waited for this moment. To understand what it felt like to be filled by a man. To feel his lips all over her body. To take him in her mouth.

She pulled his underwear down, pausing briefly to clear the hurdle of his erection. He finished the job, taking off his socks, too. When he straightened up, she held her breath.

He was gorgeous. His broad chest, the light covering of hair over the planes of his muscles. His tummy, flat, rippled, perfect. As for his sex? Spectacular. She wasn't terribly good with measurements, but he hadn't lied about his dimensions.

"Jamie? Are you going to stare at me all night?"

"Oh, no. I want to touch you, too."

He laughed again, but this time she welcomed the sound, recognizing the warmth and affection behind it. "Do you want to stand here or go to the bed?"

"The bed." She reached out, got a firm grip on his shaft, amazed at the softness of his skin and the hardness of what lay beneath, and headed toward the bed.

"Hey, that's attached."

"Well, then, come on."

"Yes, ma'am."

She released him when she got to the bed. Then she sat on the edge and maneuvered him in front of her.

Now she was eye-level with his belly button. But she didn't give a hang about that. Her focus was his male parts. She'd seen pictures, movies; read about penises; heard all the different slang names—and yet she'd never seen one in the flesh. Well, that's not true. She'd seen little boys when she baby-sat, but that was comparing apples and oranges. Or cucumbers and... gherkins.

"What's that smile for?"

"Nothing," she said. "Except that I think you've got a beautiful penis."

"Thanks. I like your labia."

She giggled, then took hold of his shaft again.

"Uh, Jamie?"

"Yeah?"

"You do realize you can do more than just hold it, right?"

"Really?"

He nodded. "All sorts of things. It's quite versatile."

"Oh?"

"Well, it doesn't whistle Dixie or anything, but it can make you feel real good."

"I want to try it all," she whispered. "Everything." She touched the very tip of him with her tongue; then, needing more of a proper taste, she licked all around the head.

He groaned and touched the back of her head with his hand. He didn't push, just touched her.

Emboldened, she started teasing him in earnest, licking from head to shaft, all the way down, and then she even teased his testicles with her tongue. His taste was a bit salty, but what she tasted most was...male. Not just any male, but Chase. Distinct, like his scent. Masculine. Intoxicating.

She found herself at the tip again, and this time instead of licking, she took him in her mouth. Although she knew that some women could open their throats all the way, she wasn't nearly that talented. But she could flick her tongue just under the glans, and she could pump his shaft while she sucked him like a lollipop. From his moans, she gathered he had no complaints. And neither did she.

It felt naughty. Scandalous. Incredible.

She wanted nothing more than to please him. To make him groan with delight. And it wouldn't hurt her feelings if he ravished her until she couldn't walk.

His hand stilled her head, and he pulled away from her. She looked up into his eyes.

"It's my turn," he said.

She didn't argue.

The next moment was something out of her dreams. He picked her up, like Richard Gere had carried Debra Winger, minus the officer's cap. He walked around the bed, and before he put her down he kissed her. It was a doozy, and she sighed with happiness. When he joined her on the bed, he looked at her from head to toe and gave her a sinful smile. A thrum of excitement started in her belly, and even before his hand went to her breast, she was trembling like a leaf.

"You're so beautiful," he whispered. "I want you so badly."

"Take me."

"Are you sure?"

She nodded. "More sure than I've ever been about anything."

"Good," he whispered, and after another brief kiss on her mouth, his lips traveled down to her chin, her neck, her chest, and then those same luscious lips closed over her right nipple. His tongue flicked her, and sensations shot through her, straight to the junction of her thighs. She felt herself moisten, and when he sucked hard, she found her hips moving without any conscious effort.

She was primed, ripe, ready for anything. He'd changed her, right from the beginning. He'd rearranged her molecules, and he'd made her understand what being a woman was all about.

Now, as he suckled her breast, as his hand meandered down her hip and her backside, she understood something else, too. This desire for him was physical, yes, but that was only the symptom, not the cause.

She wanted him to be inside her, to fill her, to complete her. She'd waited a lifetime for this moment, for this man. She ran her hand through his hair, and that brought him away from her breast. He straightened until his gaze and hers locked, and for breathless moments she saw something completely new. She saw herself in her lover's eyes. And she was beautiful.

He slid down her body until she felt his hands on her knees. Gently, he spread her legs, then moved between them. She grabbed the covers with both hands as his head lowered to her sex.

His warm breath made her tense; then his lips were on her and it was all she could do not to cry. And it just kept getting better.

He licked her, slid his tongue inside, found the magic knob and coaxed it from under its hood, and then he sucked her until she thrashed and cried out. His tongue danced, and his finger entered her, teasing, thrusting, unlocking her secrets. Thoughts vanished, the world disappeared as she writhed under him. And then her body tensed, every muscle grew taut trembling, all the feelings she'd ever felt right there where his tongue was—

She exploded.

And, in the next moment, while the fireworks were going off one after another, he was at the gates of her sex, his thick, hot manhood slipping inside.

She moved her hips up, wanting him, needing him. He moved slowly, steadily. When she looked at him, she saw the control, the cords on his neck, the concentration in his eyes. He was holding back so he wouldn't hurt her.

She didn't care. Nothing mattered except having him inside her. All the way.

"Do it," she whispered. "Please. Make love to me, Chase."

"I might hurt you."

"I don't care." She lifted her hips again. "Please, Chase. Now."

He closed his eyes for a moment, opened them again, and as she gazed at his face, he thrust into her. One long, brilliant, unbelievable push until he had stretched her beyond anything she'd known before, until he was fully inside her, until they had become one.

Tears came, but not from pain. From joy. From pleasure. From Chase.

He made slow love to her, and as he did, his gaze never wavered. They connected, not just sexually but spiritually. Something magic passed between them, and she felt as if her fate and his combined to make two new beings. Or was it only one?

She climaxed again, this time in a different way, a softer total body release. And after she finished, he started his climb. Moving faster, his muscles tense and his gaze electric, he thrust harder, harder, and then he gave a cry that was heaven and hell. She wrapped her legs around him, riding his climax, sharing the moment, loving the man.

Loving the man.

Everything changed. In the blink of an eye. On the crest of a wave. In the arms of her man.

15

CHASE STARED UP at the ceiling as Jamie slept, nestled in the crook of his arm. Now, he'd gone and done it. He'd crossed a line he'd avoided all his life. There was no couching it in softer terms, no denying the fact. He'd fallen in love.

It wasn't the sex, and yet it was. It wasn't her little striptease, yet that was when it had first hit him. Then he'd entered her and realized he never wanted to leave. He wanted to be in her, part of her, with her, forever. Only, for him, forever wasn't in the cards.

How could he do this to her? To himself? Never before had he felt so much, so fiercely. He wanted to protect her, to care for her, to give her every gift known to man. He didn't want to go to Paris or Budapest or anywhere that would take him from her side. No one had told him this was what love was like. He'd never suspected. It was consuming, blocking out the sun and the moon and the stars. It made him someone new.

Just feeling her now, her leg curled around his, her hand on his chest, her warm breath against his skin, he wanted to make love to her again. And again.

The way she looked at him, he knew it was true for her, too. She'd been bewitched, just as he had. Which meant that he was going to hurt her.

Whether today, or next week or in the hour of his death, he was going to crush her with pain. He cursed his father, his genes. For the first time since the truth had come to him, he wanted to change his destiny. He wanted to live.

"Jamie, what have you done?" he whispered, his gaze on her beautiful face. Mesmerized by her pale skin, by the way her eyelashes touched her cheeks, he yearned for something he couldn't have.

The thought of not telling her, of acting as if they had a lifetime ahead of them, was tempting. But it would be a lie, and he'd know it every day. He'd know that it was selfish—and how could he love someone so completely and care nothing for her feelings?

It wasn't fair. In fact, it was a cold, hard bitch—a cruel trick by an uncaring god.

He loved her. It wasn't something he could turn off like a faucet or pretend didn't exist. He had to make some decisions, and he had to make them soon. Before Paris. If there was going to be a Paris.

She stirred, and he wanted to make love to her again. But she was probably sore, and he didn't want to hurt her that way, either. Three times, he'd been inside her. Three times, he'd had mind-blowing climaxes. Three times, he'd watched her shudder with release.

He wanted her again, desperately, but instead he slipped out of bed, careful not to wake her. He went to the bathroom and started a bath. She'd need the warmth and the comfort after such a workout. He even added some bubble bath the hotel had provided.

After a few moments, he went back into the bedroom. She was awake, and her smile made his insides go crazy. How was it possible to feel so much in such a short time? He'd never believed love could hit him like this, like a truck going sixty miles an hour. But he'd been struck, all right.

"Do I hear a bath?"

He nodded. "For you."

She sighed, and her smile warmed him. "What time is it?"

"Three."

"P.M.?"

"Yep."

"So that's why I'm so hungry."

"While you're in the tub, I'll order food. What do you want?"

"Everything."

He laughed. "I think you need to be a little more specific."

"Eggs. Bacon. Toast. Hash browns. Pancakes. Coffee. Orange juice."

"Is that all?"

"I'll let you know."

Dammit, how was he supposed to leave this? Leave her? She was everything he hadn't known he wanted. All his dreams fulfilled.

She pushed back the covers and got up. On her way to the bathroom she stopped and kissed him. "Thank you."

"My pleasure."

Her grin made her even more exquisite. "I know. I'll be out soon."

"Don't hurry. I'll let you know when breakfast comes."

"Okay."

And then she padded to the bathroom, and he watched her naked back, entranced by her bottom and her hips and her legs and every part of her—and he wanted her. Again.

"GABBY, SLOW DOWN. Start from the beginning." Jamie sipped some tea as she brought her mind back to Gabby and her problems. It had been a difficult show. All she wanted was to go to Chase. To touch him. To make love to him. But the show must go on. Which, it suddenly occurred to her, was a crock. Who cared about a show when there was love in the air?

No. No, she did care. She loved her job. Just not as much as she loved Chase.

"He ended it," Gabby said through her tears. "He even took his CDs—and the tie I gave him for Christmas."

"Did he say anything before he left?"

Gabby sniffed. "He said he couldn't take it anymore. That I was suffocating him."

Jamie sighed. "I'm so sorry, honey. I know it must hurt like the devil."

"You do?"

"More than you can imagine. I can't think of anything tougher than to love someone with all your heart and not have that love returned."

Gabby's sniffle turned to sobs. For a moment, Jamie just let her weep. Then, softly, she said, "Gabby, there are lessons here. Maybe you can't see them today, but when you're ready, we can talk about them. You're going to find true love, but only if you can learn from this and not make the same mistakes."

"I know. I wanted too much."

"Not too much. Just from the wrong source. You have to be whole before you can share yourself. You have to make yourself happy."

"I'll never be happy again."

"You will. I promise."

"Thanks, Dr. Jamie. And sorry about that thing with Chase."

"No need to be sorry. I won."

"I don't know. You could have made love to him. You could have had the time of your life, but you didn't. That doesn't sound like winning to me."

Jamie wondered if she should tell her listeners the whole truth. No, not now, not tonight. But she knew her show wouldn't be the same after tonight. She wouldn't change the format, but she wouldn't be the same therapist. She saw now how pompous she had been in her posturing. Love wasn't something that could be quantified. Rules were for fools and virgins.

"I'll have to think about that, Gabby. Thanks. This is Dr. Jamie, and we're talking about sex."

MARCY SLIPPED into the booth across from Chase, and a moment later the waitress brought coffee. She was bursting with curiosity. Why had Chase asked to see her, and what was with all the hush-hush business?

He took a sip of coffee, then looked her straight in the eye. "I need to know you won't ever say anything about this conversation to anyone, ever."

"Okay."

"I mean it. I won't talk unless I have your word."

"You do."

He sighed, and Marcy noted how tired he looked. But still gorgeous. Her mind bounced to her man, Ted. Only, he wasn't hers. Not the way she wanted him. They'd had dinner. And after a while, she'd actually had fun. But he hadn't even tried to kiss her good-night. She hated the word *platonic*. It didn't say nearly enough about the ache in her heart.

"Jamie and I—" Chase began. He closed his mouth

for a moment, then started again. "Jamie and I have a problem."

"Yes?"

"I can't tell you everything, but there are some things..."

"What?"

"Damn. I don't know how to say this, so I'm just going to talk. Jamie and I—we've, um, I've fallen in love with her."

"That's wonderful."

"No, it isn't."

"Why not?"

"It just shouldn't have happened. That's all."

"Oh, no. That's not enough. Come on, Chase. Spill it."

"You know about my father, right?"

She nodded. "He owned the station."

"And he died at thirty-five."

"I'm sorry. I had no idea he was that young."

"My grandfather died at thirty-five. And his father died at thirty-four. You get the picture?"

"Is it a heart ailment? A congenital defect?"

He shrugged. "The doctors don't know why. They can't see anything wrong, and, believe me, I've had every test in the book."

"But you still think you're going to die, like them."

"Wouldn't you?"

"I don't know."

"I do. Destiny is a hard thing to face when it doesn't hold anything good."

"But you love Jamie, right?"

"Which is the problem. Which is why I'm here. You need to look after her."

"Why?"

"Didn't you hear me?"

"Yeah. You think you're gonna die. I have news for you, Chase. No one gets out of this alive. We're all gonna die."

"Not in the next three years."

"How do you know? I might walk out of here and get hit by a bus."

"Yeah, but—"

"The truth is, you don't know what's going to happen. You might die at thirty-five or a hundred-and-five. You don't know until you go."

"But if I do go in a couple of years, what will that do to Jamie?"

"You're worried about something that might or might not happen in two years? Good God, man, you are gorgeous but you're not very bright."

"Hey—"

"You know what you have? Today. That's all. Yesterday is gone, and there isn't a thing you can do to change it. Tomorrow is a maybe, a complete unknown. So all that matters is now, right now. So you have a couple of choices. You can waste today thinking about a tomorrow you can't see, or you can live right here, right now, for all you're worth."

"You don't get it."

"I do. More than you can know. My mother had Alzheimer's, Chase. I watched a vibrant, lovely, loving woman become a stranger who didn't even know my name. And I thought about all the days I'd wasted with her. When we could have been talking and laughing and just being with each other. I can never get that back. I wasted my todays just like you are doing. I was a fool."

"There's something else."

"Uh-oh."

"It's about Jamie."

She waited, trying not to nudge him into talking faster. "She's, she was… Damn, I don't know if I should tell you. But I really think she needs a friend and, well…"

"If you don't tell me now, I'm going to strangle you."

"Oh, crap. Jamie was…a virgin."

"Pardon me?"

He nodded. "As pure as the driven snow."

"You're lying."

He shook his head, and she knew it was the truth. But how could that be? "She's Dr. Jamie."

He nodded. "Yep. And she was ready to quit because she felt like a fraud. This whole thing, it's been rough on her. I can't help her, but you can."

"Oh man. But it makes some kind of weird sense, you know? Things I couldn't quite put together. Holy— I'm assuming from your use of the past tense that she's no longer?"

"Right."

"So what's the problem?"

"I can't shake the feeling I've done something wrong, something that will hurt her. It wasn't my place—"

"Did you force her?"

"No. Jeez."

"So, she was willing and consenting?"

"Yes."

"So, it's not your problem, unless you totally sucked at it."

His grin said he didn't think so. But then, he was a guy, and sometimes they didn't see so clearly.

"Okay, then. You made love with a beautiful woman who wanted to make love to you. You fell in love with this woman and, from what you say, she fell in love right back. The only fly in the ointment is a future no one can predict. Unlike the rest of us who know every detail of what's going to happen for the rest of our lives."

"All right. I hear you."

"Do you?"

"I watched my mother fall apart after my father died. We nearly didn't make it."

"But you did. And so did your mother. Tell me, have you ever asked her if she'd have been happier if she'd never loved your father?"

He shook his head. "No."

"Ask her. I already know the answer."

He didn't say anything for a long time. Then he got his wallet, left several bills on the table and stood. "Thanks, Marcy."

"You're welcome."

"I'm glad you're Jamie's friend."

She smiled as he walked away, and she wondered if she'd ever be loved by a man like Chase. If she'd ever be loved at all.

Jamie walked out of the elevator, and the world shifted one degree to the right. To the perfect. Chase was at her apartment door.

She hurried—hell, she ran—and she didn't even warn him when she jumped into his arms, wrapped her legs around him and kissed him senseless. He staggered, but only for a few seconds. Then he held her tight and kissed her back.

She'd memorized his scent. It was an aphrodisiac, a

balm to her soul, a catalyst for her awakening. She'd thought about him all night, and if he hadn't been there, she'd have hunted him down.

He broke the kiss, making her moan, but then he smiled. "You're light as a feather, and normally I could do this for several days, but I have to use the facilities, if you get my drift."

She sighed dramatically. "Oh, okay. I suppose I could let you go. But a real man would have lasted another ten minutes at least."

"No, that would have been a real stupid man."

She slid down until her feet were on the floor, then unlocked her door. Chase scooted past her, and although she knew it was absolutely ridiculous, she felt all warm and fuzzy that they had joked about something so personal, just like a real couple.

But were they? She hadn't asked yet. Maybe because she didn't want to know. He could still leave. He could break her heart this very night. On the other hand...

She went into the kitchen to make some iced tea, and realized she didn't know if Chase liked tea or not. What if he was a beer man? She didn't have beer.

There was so much to learn about him. She didn't know anything about his family, his childhood. Why he'd gotten involved with racing and, for heaven's sake, why he didn't live in an apartment like a normal person. He could certainly afford it.

Who was this man who'd stolen her heart? Tonight, she'd find out.

His boots across her wood floor revved up her engine, and then his arms were around her waist and she leaned against his strong chest.

"Hey, beautiful," he whispered.

"Hey, handsome."

His hands moved to her breasts, and he cupped them possessively. She felt tingly. "What are you making?"

"Tea. Iced tea. Do you like it? I think I have some soda. Or maybe not. There might be a bottle of wine in the back of the fridge. Or I could go to the market—"

He spun her around. "I think I know what went wrong."

"Huh?"

"I should have kissed you immediately."

Her heart melted. "Exactly."

Once more, she was in his arms, but this time she kissed him more leisurely. They weren't going anywhere. And as for finding out about his family? That could wait. Most definitely.

Chase couldn't believe how good she felt, how she excited him so quickly. He'd meant to talk to her, to figure out together what they were going to do next. But there was no talking possible, not until he'd sunk deep inside her, until he'd made her thrash and scream, until they'd both come. And come again.

He led her toward her bedroom. Even holding her hand made him crazy. Damn, he'd thought he understood sex, but he hadn't. Sure, he knew what part went where, but he'd never guessed that it could be this fine, this important. Who knew that caring more about her than himself would lead to the most intense release he'd ever known?

"Chase?"

"Hmm?"

"Am I supposed to undress you?"

He grinned. "Not unless you want to."

"I'd rather we just hurried."

"Really, now," he said, drawing the words out

slowly. He sat down on the edge of her bed, stuck his hands in his pockets, which wasn't all that easy considering his raging hard-on, and gave her a puzzled look. "You want us to hurry? Is that what you're saying?"

"Yes."

"Hmm."

"Chase!"

"Yeah?" he drawled.

"What are you doing?"

"Making you nuts."

She shook her head. "And you're doing a terrific job. I'm taking off all my clothes right now, and then I'm getting in the bed and I'm going to have sex. If you want to join me, that's fine."

"And if I don't?"

"Then, honey, it would be your loss."

He reached up, grabbed his shirt in his fists and ripped it open, sending buttons flying across the room.

Jamie laughed, really laughed, and it turned out that he got naked before she did. Then he had to help her unhook her bra and slip off her panties. He didn't mind.

And when she trailed kisses down his chest and took him in her mouth, he had to use all his control not to come in seconds. When he couldn't stand the pleasure anymore, he lifted her by the shoulders and spread her on the bed. He kissed her over and over as his hands slid down to her sex, and then he explored her like a blind man reading braille, every wrinkle and fold and crevice, and her pleasure became his pleasure.

After a long, long time, she took the lead, and she had him flat on his back. She straddled him, and their eyes met. She lowered herself inch by slow inch, then she did the most amazing thing. She moved her body like a belly dancer would, undulating, squeezing, swaying over him in a way designed to make him mad with lust.

He felt the wave build, and she somehow knew, and her rhythm changed. No more tricks or teasing. She balanced herself on her feet, braced her arms on his chest, and she rode him until he wanted to yell. Full strokes, until only the tip was inside her, then down to the base, over and over, so tight, so hot, he couldn't think, couldn't see. But he could feel.

He thrust his hips up to meet her, and then he came so hard he almost blacked out. He heard his own cry as if from a distance, his whole focus, every part of him, centered on their connection.

When he came back to earth, she was still on top, and he was still inside her. She smiled a woman's smile, knowing exactly what she'd done to him.

"So you say you've never done this before?" he asked.

She shook her head. "Well, except for last night."

"Fair enough."

"What's that smile for?"

"I was just wondering what you'll be like when you get good at this."

She smiled as she leaned forward, then she kissed him. He never wanted the moment to end. He had had enough of reality. Now he wanted ecstasy, and he wanted it forever.

His intention was to tell her everything. But, coward that he was, he didn't.

Tomorrow. Tomorrow would be for hard truth. Tonight would be for magic.

SHE TIPTOED OUT of the bedroom and closed the door. He needed to sleep some more. So did she, but that wasn't going to happen. Since she'd already grabbed a shower, she might as well get something to eat. It made sense to her that lovers died in each other's arms—they probably just screwed each other to death. That wasn't going to happen to them. She figured she'd wake up Chase with a big old omelette and some toast, and if she wasn't mistaken, there was some bacon in the crisper.

But first she'd grab the paper. She undid the locks as quietly as she could, then opened the door a smidge. As always, the *Times* and the *Post* were side by side at her door. She grabbed them, hoping no one would walk by; she had on Chase's shirt, and it had no buttons. Once inside, she locked the door again and headed for the kitchen.

She didn't open the paper until the eggs were in the pan and the bacon was cooking in the microwave. Why she chose to look at the *Post* first was a mystery. It wasn't her usual habit. In fact, she always looked at the *Times*. But not this afternoon.

She stood by the table, juice in one hand, and unfolded the paper. For a moment, she didn't understand the headline. She certainly didn't think it was about her. Not until she saw the picture of Chase, the picture of her.

Her gaze moved back to the bold words, Sex Doctor a Virgin! And then the byline, Darlene Whittaker.

The juice glass slipped from her hand and broke into a million pieces, right along with her heart.

16

JAMIE HAD TO SIT DOWN, or else she would fall down. God, how could he? She'd thought she knew him, but it was all a charade. The betrayal was like a fatal knife wound killing her over and over again.

Chase had never loved her. She didn't even know if he liked her. And she would have given up the world for him.

Burying her head in her hands, the tears came, her grief made tangible. It wasn't enough. She needed to do something, hurt someone, rail at God. But she couldn't, not with him in the other room.

How could she have been so stupid, so wrong? My God, she had no business telling anyone on earth what to do. How could she give advice when she was such an unbelievable moron?

She thought back to the way he'd laughed at her impromptu striptease. To know the laughter had been real, that it wasn't affectionate or loving in any way, made her want to crawl under a rock and die. Why had he come to see her last night—after his mission had been accomplished?

Was it to rub salt in the wound? To dig up more of her secret past? Or was she just a convenient hole before he went off to Paris?

She stood up, rage filling her with the need for revenge. She'd go in the bedroom. Confront him with his lies. Tell him… Tell him what? That he had crippled her? That she'd fallen for all of his honeyed words? That she was the biggest fool in America?

It was too much, too new for her to speak with any clarity. She wanted him out of here so she could curl up in the fetal position and weep until there were no more tears. Maybe later, maybe after she'd cried herself a river, she'd be able to ask him why. How he could be so evil. What he got for making such a fool of her.

To think he and Whittaker were in cahoots the whole time. She moaned with the humiliation. Of course she'd lose her job, but she'd also lose the respect of her peers, her listeners and everyone else that mattered to her.

If only she'd been strong. If she'd stuck to her guns. If she hadn't been duped by his smile, his voice, the way he looked at her.

Her world had crashed around her, and the only thing she could blame was her own naiveté.

She sprang from her chair, a wave of panic sending her into the living room and to her bedroom door. She must get out. Now. God forbid he should wake up. But where could she go?

Marcy. She'd talk to Marcy, and her friend would help her see. What time was it? Two in the afternoon. Wherever Marcy was, she'd have her cell phone with her. The only thing Jamie had to do was somehow get her clothes without waking Chase, and get the hell out of here.

Opening the door slowly, she saw that he was still sleeping the sleep of the innocent. The bastard. On tiptoes, she walked in, gathered up her clothes, her shoes, her purse. Then, without disturbing him, she walked away and closed the door behind her. With luck, it would be the last time she'd ever see him.

Five minutes later, she was dressed. Her hair was a nightmare and she wasn't wearing makeup, but she didn't care. She couldn't be here, not another second.

When she reached the front door, her gaze went back to the bedroom. Half an hour ago, she'd been walking ten feet off the ground. Her world had been shiny and perfect. Now, she felt like she'd been hit by a speeding train. Thanks, Chase.

"CALM DOWN, I can't understand you," said Marcy.

Chase rubbed the sleep out of his eyes and stared at the newspaper headline again. It still turned his stomach. "Darlene Whittaker wrote a front page story for the *Post*. Want to hear the headline? 'Sex Doctor a Virgin.' Want to hear the line after that? 'How her hoax will change radio forever.'"

"My God."

"Is that all you can say?" He crumpled the paper in his hand, wishing it were Darlene's neck. Or Marcy's.

"What do you want me to say? It's devastating."

"Then, why did you do it?"

"What?"

"Marcy, I didn't tell Darlene. That leaves you and Jamie. Considering she ran out of her own apartment, I don't think she's the main suspect."

"Chase, watch it. You don't want to say something you'll regret."

"You're telling me you didn't call Darlene?"

"I'm telling you exactly that. I haven't opened my mouth, not to a living soul."

Something told him she was telling the truth, which

meant that somehow, someone else had found out about Jamie. "Do you think Jamie could have told someone?"

"She wouldn't have called Darlene Whittaker if the reporter was the last person on earth."

"I don't mean Darlene. I mean anyone. An old friend. Someone at the station. Someone she thought she could trust."

"I can't tell you that. But for what it's worth, I'm probably her closest friend and I knew nothing. I was stunned when you told me."

"You were?"

"Well, of course. What did you think?"

"I don't know. You were pretty cool."

"I get paid to be pretty cool."

"Shit." He sat down hard. "She must think it was me."

"Probably."

"So how do I clear myself? She'll never believe me."

"She will, Chase, if what you told me was true. If you love her, she'll know it. Maybe not immediately, but she'll come around."

"Are you sure?"

"I hope so. Damn, I hated that bitch Whittaker from the moment I saw her."

Chase stood, his thoughts tumbling on top of each other. "Marcy, find her. Take care of her. I've got something to do. But whatever you do, make her do her show tonight."

"Wait—"

He didn't. He was going to make sure Jamie knew he hadn't told about her. And he was going to get a retraction in the paper. No one messed with someone he cared about. Not if they expected to keep breathing.

JAMIE AVOIDED almost everyone on her trek to the office. Everyone except the news vendor on the corner. He grinned at her as if they'd shared a joke. "Hey, is what they say in the paper true? You still a virgin, Doc?"

She didn't answer him, afraid she'd burst into hysterics right there on 57th Street. Instead, she walked as quickly as she could inside the building, went right to the emporium on the ground floor and bought a rather ugly, old-fashioned men's rain hat. It cost almost forty dollars, but Jamie didn't care. If she could have, she would have bought a tent to hide under.

The thing she'd feared most had come to pass. To make matters worse, the truth being revealed turned out not to be the most devastating event in her life. That honor went to Chase Newman's deception. She'd finally dared to love, to trust. And he'd squished her under his boot heel like an ant.

Shoving her change in her pocket, she plopped the hat on her head and brought it down over her eyes so that she could barely see. But then, people could barely see her, so that was fine.

Her disguise worked all the way to her office. Of course, it helped that no one was in the reception area. She prayed for Marcy, who hadn't answered her phone, to be in her office. And for a change, her prayer was answered.

Marcy rose from her desk, and from the look on her face, Jamie knew she'd read the story.

She flew into the older woman's arms, and for a long time, she had no idea how long, she wept, bawled like a baby. Wave after wave of pain washed over her, and she was helpless to stop it.

Marcy rocked her back and forth, calming her with quiet compassion until Jamie could breathe again.

"I don't understand," she said, her voice laden with tears. "How could he? I fell in love with him and he—"

"You don't know that," Marcy said. "He might not have had anything to do with it."

"No one else knew. No one on the planet."

"Honey, there could be another explanation. Even if you can't see it right now. What you have to look at is what you know about Chase. Did he ever behave in a way that would even suggest he could do something this heinous?"

"Marcy, I've only known him a week. He could be Jack the Ripper, for all I know."

Marcy pushed her back to arm's length and forced Jamie to meet her gaze. "That's a lie, and you know it."

"How is it a lie?"

"Because you're incredibly intuitive. Why do you think you're so brilliant at what you do? You read people, Jamie, like I read a book. You see where they need confidence, or where they've been wounded. You can't fake that. Radio audiences are too smart for that."

"Radio audiences? I don't have any, not anymore. Everything I love was wiped out with a headline. I'm a fraud, Marcy, and it's time you knew it. I have no business trying to help people. What the hell do I know? I believed in Chase."

"I still believe in Chase."

"Why?"

"Because I'm pretty damn intuitive myself. And I think he loves you and he wouldn't ever hurt you."

"No? Okay, aside from the whole life-altering betrayal thing, what about Paris? Budapest? He's out of here. On the next plane. What does that say about his love for me?"

"You don't know that, either."

"Marcy, who's your friend, him or me? Why are you trying to protect him?"

"Because you're my friend. And I think you care a great deal about Chase, and the same is true for him."

"Right. He cares for Chase, too."

"Stop it."

"Why? He told Darlene Whittaker the most awful secret of my life!"

"Why is it so awful?"

Jamie stopped. "What?"

"Why is your being a virgin so awful? Lots of people are. It's not that big a deal."

"Tell that to Lorraine or Gabby. These people trusted me."

"So? They still do."

"That's not possible. I betrayed them. How can they get advice on sex from someone who's never had sex?"

"Jamie, honey, what you talk to them about isn't sex. It's about being a person. Feelings. Emotions. How to handle the scary business of life."

"Exactly. And I don't have any idea how to handle life."

"Yes, you do. Your gift hasn't been diminished. In fact, I bet there are hundreds and hundreds of women who'll applaud your decision to wait."

Jamie shook her head. "Yeah, I wasn't satisfied with

sleeping with any son of a bitch. I waited until I found *the* son of a bitch.''

''Will you at least give him a chance? Let him tell you his side of the story?''

''No. The evidence is in black and white. He did this thing to me, and I'm sorry, Marcy, but it's unforgivable.''

''I think you're making a mistake.''

''It wouldn't be the first time.''

CHASE RODE UP to Darlene's apartment building and stepped off his bike. She was home, he knew that. He also knew quite a number of other things about her. The past few hours had been hectic but fascinating. He'd never dreamed so many of his father's old friends would help. And each one had a story to tell, a memory to share. His father, even in his short life, had touched a hell of a lot of people.

But that wasn't the central issue. Darlene needed a lesson in ethics, and he was just the man to teach her.

JAMIE SIPPED HER TEA curled up in Marcy's leather chair, hiding from the rest of the world. She was supposed to go on the air in a few hours, but she didn't see how. She was a wreck.

Her mind kept slinking over to Marcy's side, trying to conceive of some way Chase could be innocent. But it was dangerous ground, like walking in quicksand. If she continued to harbor the slightest doubt about his guilt, then she was likely to let down her defenses—and then she was done for. Chase was too slick, too charming. And the truth was, she wanted to believe him. She wanted everything to be the way it was this morning. When he'd made slow love to her. The look in his eyes—

No, no, no. She couldn't go there. It would just start her crying again, and she didn't have the strength.

The sound of someone entering Marcy's outer office distracted her, and she sighed, staring at the slightly open door, waiting for her friend to come in. Only, she didn't. Just as Jamie was going to get up to investigate, she heard someone else come through the outer door.

"Hey, Marcy."

That was Ted's voice.

"Hello."

"You wanted to see me?"

Marcy cleared her throat. "I did."

"Here I am. Want to—"

"No. I want to stay right here, because if I don't spit this out this second, I never will."

"What?"

Jamie leaned forward, straining to hear, even though she knew it was none of her business. Marcy's voice sounded so...odd.

"I wanted you to know that when I asked you out to dinner, it wasn't as a friend."

"No?"

"Uh-uh."

"What did you ask me out for?"

"Damn. I'm sorry, I'm probably going to embarrass the hell out of you. I never dreamed I'd say anything like this, but my friend, she's going through a lot right now because she doesn't know the real story, and I don't want to miss out on something that could be totally terrific because I was a chicken, so I'm just going to say it, and you don't have to worry, if it's no, I'll under—"

Marcy's voice stopped mid-word. But, if Jamie wasn't mistaken, there were still signs of life coming from the other room. Kissing sounds. Scratch that. *Major* kissing sounds.

After an embarrassingly long time, she heard a deep intake of breath and a nervous cough.

"Why didn't you tell me?" Marcy asked.

"I wasn't sure how you felt."

"Me? Are you kidding?"

He shook his head. "I haven't done this in a while. I wasn't sure I was reading the signals correctly. I've been trying to get up my nerve to talk to you."

"Oh."

He laughed softly. "Thank you."

"Me? For what?"

"For being so brave. Imagine all the time and misery we've saved because you were willing to put yourself out there. No wonder I'm crazy about you."

"Really?"

Marcy's voice was high-pitched, breathy, and so full of happiness that Jamie wanted to cry. For her friend. Okay, so some of it was jealousy, but the lion's share wasn't. She just kinda wished she couldn't hear all the smooching. She loved Marcy, but not that much.

There was no way to sneak out. She'd have to wait until they finished. She might as well use the time to think. About Ted and Marcy. About bravery. About missed connections.

"IS IT TRUE?"

Jamie inhaled, closed her eyes and prayed for the right words. "It was true, Lorraine. It's not true any longer."

"You mean, you lost the bet?"

The bet? Who cared about that? She'd just admitted that she'd had no personal sexual experience while she was counseling on the air, and her listeners were concerned about the bet?

"Dr. Jamie?"

"No, Lorraine. I didn't lose. Because I walked into the situation with my eyes open. There was no seduction, no trickery. I'm fully responsible for my own actions."

"Wow. So, uh, was he, you know, as good as he looks?"

Jamie felt as if she'd been punched. But she'd made the decision to answer any questions honestly. To speak only the truth, whatever the repercussions. "He was."

"Man, that is so cool."

"Are you telling me you're not upset about my, uh, situation?"

"You mean the article?"

"Yes."

"I can't believe you got to be as old as you did without doing the deed, but, no, why should it bother me?"

"Because I've given you advice."

"So has my priest. Your advice is better."

"Oh."

"You sound disappointed. Did you want me to be upset?"

"No," she said, but she had to wonder if that was the absolute truth. "I just felt so guilty. Now, I'm feeling pretty foolish."

"I have someone you can call," Lorraine said. "Her name is Dr. Jamie, and she's the best. She helped me see that I'm doing the best I can with what I've got, as long as I'm taking responsibility for my actions. That I need to be true to my heart, and that I need balance in my life.''

Jamie's eyes burned with tears that she struggled to hold back. ''Thank you,'' she whispered. ''More than you'll ever know. This is Dr. Jamie, and we're talking about life.''

Cujo took his cue, and Jamie leaned back in her chair, trying to figure out what had just happened. She'd been on the air for almost an hour with three different women. Not one had cared a whit about her virginity. They were curious about her reactions to her first time, and, despite her vow to be honest, she wasn't able to talk about that. Not that she lied. She just explained that she wasn't ready for the discussion yet.

The pain was so acute, maybe she'd never be ready. But then, how else could she turn this fiasco into something positive? There was a lesson here. She just wondered what it was.

At least she still had her show. Which was a bloody miracle. Marcy had clocked in a record number of calls, and Fred had been using the *Post* article to generate more publicity. So, was she nuts for feeling as if she'd been a fraud? That she owed everyone an apology?

The commercials were almost over, and for that she was grateful. Too much time to think led her straight down the tubes. She'd heard so many good things about Chase from people who'd known him for years. How could that be? Was it possible Marcy was right?

Four, three, two... ''We're back.'' She scooted closer to the mike. ''Our next caller is—''

''Dr. Jamie?''

At Marcy's voice, Jamie looked up at the window.

Her producer rarely interrupted her show, especially not seconds after a commercial break. "Yes?"

"Why don't we talk to our next caller after we visit with our guest?"

Even before the door to her booth opened, Jamie knew it was Chase. She stood, wanting to run and hide, but there was only the one door. How could Marcy betray her, too?

Astonishingly, it wasn't Chase who walked in. Her old nemesis Darlene Whittaker had come back to the scene of the crime. Oh, perfect. Jamie would have given just about anything to disappear from the face of the earth right now. Her anger felt like a burning coal in her stomach, and if she'd known the first thing about martial arts, Whittaker would be on her butt by now.

"Jamie?"

Marcy's voice reminded her she was on the air. "Our guest is none other than Darlene Whittaker. Normally, Darlene writes magazine articles, but lately she's been moonlighting for the *New York Post*. How nice to see you, Darlene."

The woman of the moment didn't seem very happy to be there. Where Jamie had expected gloating, she saw only discomfort. Jamie felt no sympathy.

"I'm, uh, sorry about all this."

"Right. So, tell me, did you and Chase have this all planned out before you came to the station that night? Or was it an impromptu deal?"

"Chase didn't know."

"Uh-huh."

Whittaker, pale in another black dress, this one boxier than the last, her hair pulled back in a tortoiseshell clip, swallowed, then turned for a quick glance at the door behind her. "He didn't."

"Want to tell me how you got this little tidbit of a headline?"

"I had someone planted in the coffee shop across the street."

"Someone?"

She nodded miserably. "He was there in case anyone from the station came in. He was supposed to eavesdrop. See if he could get any dirt."

"He must have gotten pretty sick of their apple pie."

"He wasn't there all the time. He knew when anyone from your show had a break. He timed it well, and he had one of the waitresses call. One of those times, he hit pay dirt."

"All for little ol' me?"

"Look, I'm sorry, okay?"

"Why?"

She didn't answer for a long while. Jamie just sat still and waited.

"You want the truth?"

Jamie nodded.

"Not because I ran the story, but because it backfired. No one cares. The paper has gotten hundreds of calls. *Vanity Fair* wants to pull me and assign another writer to do the article on you."

"I see."

"Can I go now?"

"No. Why are you here, Darlene? You don't want to be."

"You know."

"Tell me."

"Chase. He brought me down here. He wanted you to know he didn't spill the beans intentionally."

Jamie's relief should have been complete, but there

was still one piece missing. She looked at Marcy. "Send him in, okay?"

Marcy nodded.

"You can go," Jamie told Whittaker.

The woman didn't need a second invitation. The door swung open, she dashed out, and Chase walked in. God, her heart went crazy, beating as if it wanted to hop out of her chest. She could hardly gather a breath, and dammit if she didn't start crying again. He hadn't told, at least not directly.

He held out his arms to her, but she stepped back. "Wait."

He let his arms drop. "What is it?"

"I need to know. Someone overheard you in the coffee shop. Who were you talking to, and why on earth would my virginity be part of the discussion?"

Chase stole a glance at Marcy, then his gaze came back to Jamie. "I was talking to your producer," he said. "And, even though it was a confidence, I needed her to know all the facts before I made my final decision."

"What decision?"

"In a minute. Marcy and I talked a lot that afternoon, and all either of us wanted was your happiness. My God, you have to believe that."

"I'd like to." He stepped closer, and this time she didn't back away. His dark, soulful eyes made her want to run to his arms. But she couldn't, not until this was all cleared up.

"Marcy was helping me decide whether I should stay or go. Leaving was pretty much the only option I could see. I never meant to care for you."

"Remarkably, this isn't making me feel better."

"Give it another minute. See, there was something I hadn't told you, something big."

"Do I really need to hear this?"

"Yeah, you do. Jamie, my father died at thirty-five. My grandfather, my great-grandfather, they all died around that age."

"Is it a medical syndrome?"

"Not that they're aware of. But my mother, she called it the Newman curse. She's always been pretty convinced I would go the way of the rest of the men in my family."

"And?"

"And I'd seen what happened to her, to me, when my father died. I didn't want to put you through it."

"Is it a sure thing? No question, you're gonna go in three years?"

He shook his head. "But it's a damn strong possibility."

"And you weren't sure I'd want you under the circumstances."

"That's about right."

"You should have asked me."

"I know."

She made the move this time. Right up to him, so she had to lean her head back to make eye contact. "Chase, I love you."

"I know."

"And I think you feel the same way about me."

"I do."

"So what the hell is the problem? If I lose you, it'll be horrible, but infinitely better than if I'd never had you at all."

"Are you sure?"

She sighed. "You love me, right?"

He nodded.

''So reverse the situation. If I were the one with the supposed curse, would you want me to leave today?''

His arms went around her back and he pulled her close. ''Not on your life.''

''Yours, either.''

''It might really happen, you know. This isn't a joke.''

''I'll deal with it, either way, any way. But I'm still not sure why you told Marcy—''

''I told her because I wasn't sure of the right thing to do. Marcy is your closest friend. I trusted her judgment. And I wanted her to look out for you.''

''What did she say?''

''She said I should stop being a damn fool. That if we love each other, that's all that matters.''

''Smart cookie, that Marcy.''

He nodded. ''I wonder if she's smart enough to find a replacement for you.''

''What?''

''Because I'm stealing you right here and right now. You're coming with me, and I'll tell you what we're gonna do.''

''Yes?''

''We're gonna talk about love.''

''Okay.''

''And then we're gonna do something about sex.''

''Okay.''

''And then—''

''Wait,'' she said, putting her finger to his lips. ''Let's save the rest for just us.''

''Deal.'' Then he leaned down and kissed her. The man who'd lied for her, fought for her honor, been so concerned about her well-being that he was willing to walk away, kissed her.

She kissed him back with all her heart and all her happiness. Just as she'd known in some deep, secret place that he was going to be the one, she also knew she'd have him for a long, long time.

Forever, no matter what.

He pulled back, took her hand and tugged her toward the door. She just had enough time to toss her headphones to Ted before she was swept down the hall and into the elevator. When the doors hissed shut, Chase did something *very* naughty and *very* wonderful.

She was the one to press the emergency stop.

Epilogue

Seven years later...

"HELLO, EVERYONE. Good morning. It's Dr. Jamie, and we're talking about life. My first guest this morning is none other than my incredible husband, Chase. Are you there?"

"Yep."

"Happy birthday, sweetie. For those who don't know, today is Chase's thirty-eighth birthday."

"Thanks."

"Why don't you tell the listeners what we did to celebrate?"

He laughed and, as always, even after all these years, it made her stomach do flip-flops. "We went to the doctor."

"And?"

"We got me a complete physical."

"Right. And what was the outcome?"

"I'm healthy as a horse."

She grinned. "Now I'll tell you about your other present."

"What would that be?"

"Tonight, Marcy and Ted are going to pick up the kids for dinner, and they're going to watch them all night long."

"Oh?"

"And I'm going to..."

"What?"

She laughed. "Sorry. I'll just have to show you. But I will give you a hint. The last time you saw me do this thing, you couldn't stop laughing."

He was quiet for several seconds. "Oh, really?"

"This time, I don't think you'll be laughing so hard."

"Jamie, have you had lessons?"

"You'll have to find out. And, my dear listeners, I just want you to know that while sex is wonderful, healthy, normal and exciting, it's love that makes the world go around. This is Dr. Jamie, encouraging you all to go for it..."

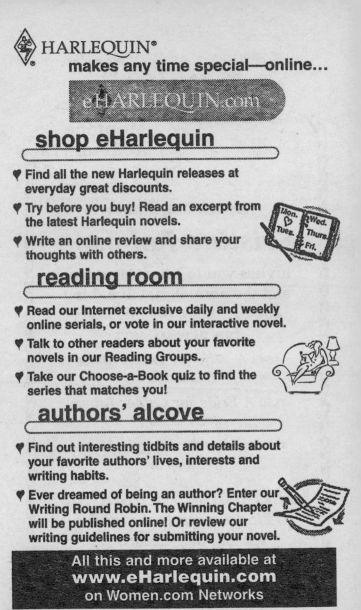